BLUE RIDGE BILLY

# Other Books by Lois Lenski

*Autobiographical*

A LITTLE GIRL OF NINETEEN HUNDRED

*Historical*

PHEBE FAIRCHILD, HER BOOK
A-GOING TO THE WESTWARD
BOUND GIRL OF COBBLE HILL
OCEAN-BORN MARY
INDIAN CAPTIVE
BLUEBERRY CORNERS
PURITAN ADVENTURE

*Regional*

BAYOU SUZETTE
STRAWBERRY GIRL
BLUE RIDGE BILLY
JUDY'S JOURNEY
BOOM TOWN BOY
COTTON IN MY SACK
TEXAS TOMBOY
PRAIRIE SCHOOL
MAMA HATTIE'S GIRL
CORN FARM BOY
SAN FRANCISCO BOY
FLOOD FRIDAY
HOUSEBOAT GIRL
COAL CAMP GIRL

BLUE RIDGE BILLY

# Other Books by Lois Lenski

## *Autobiographical*

A LITTLE GIRL OF NINETEEN HUNDRED

## *Historical*

PHEBE FAIRCHILD, HER BOOK
A-GOING TO THE WESTWARD
BOUND GIRL OF COBBLE HILL
OCEAN-BORN MARY
INDIAN CAPTIVE
BLUEBERRY CORNERS
PURITAN ADVENTURE

## *Regional*

BAYOU SUZETTE
STRAWBERRY GIRL
BLUE RIDGE BILLY
JUDY'S JOURNEY
BOOM TOWN BOY
COTTON IN MY SACK
TEXAS TOMBOY
PRAIRIE SCHOOL
MAMA HATTIE'S GIRL
CORN FARM BOY
SAN FRANCISCO BOY
FLOOD FRIDAY
HOUSEBOAT GIRL
COAL CAMP GIRL

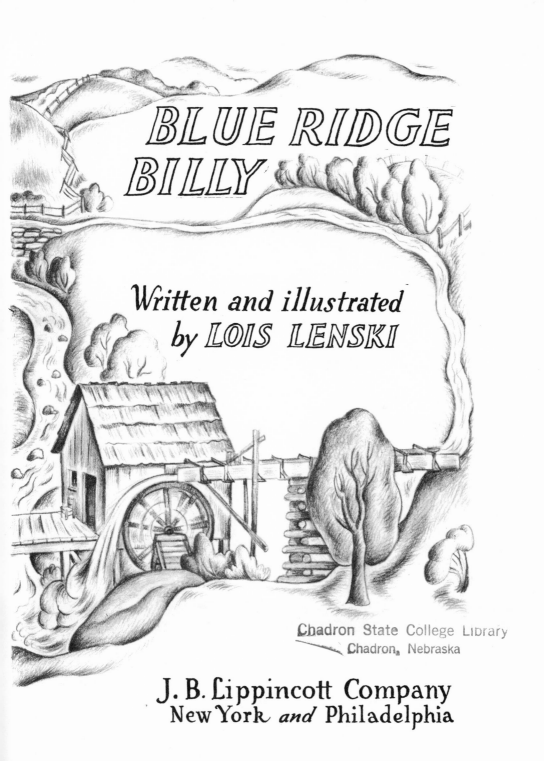

# BLUE RIDGE BILLY

Written and illustrated
by LOIS LENSKI

J. B. Lippincott Company
New York *and* Philadelphia

Tenth Printing

Library of Congress catalog card number 46-6400

*For*
*Bad Penny*
*on*
*Tumbling Creek*

VIRGINIA

Bristol Va.-Tenn.

TENNESSEE

Mt. City

Ashe
Solitude County

Peak &
Three-Top

Boone

Yadkin River

Mountains

North
Wilkesboro

To Greensboro

Blue Ridge

N

A Map of
NORTH CAROLINA

W ← → E

showing Solitude ◉

in Ashe County

○ Asheville

Va.

Tenn.

North Carolina

○ Asheville

○ Raleigh

S.C.

Ga.

Atlantic Ocean

S

# CONTENTS

# *Foreword*

## SEEING OTHERS AS OURSELVES

What a wonderful country ours is! Wherever you go, you can always find new scenes, people with new customs and habits and different ways of making a living from those you have seen in other regions.

I think the artist is a specially privileged person, because always he sees the world spread out like a stage before him, a play being enacted for his own special benefit. He approaches it objectively, with all his senses sharpened, filled with "a great awareness"—a sensitivity like that of a human camera, to make a record of it. He looks not for those things which are the same or similar to his own past experience, but for differences; he forgets himself and identifies himself with the new scene and its activities.

The approach of the artist and the writer is not exactly the same. An artist looks at the outward surface of things. He is primarily interested in what meets the eye. He looks for beauty, character, action, design and pattern, but he rarely goes more than skin-deep. A writer, on the other hand, has to understand reasons and motives. With all the inquisitiveness of a four-year-old, he keeps asking, "Why? Why? Why?" He must find out the hidden meanings of all he sees and hears.

What fun it is to explore a new and unknown world, full of limitless possibilities—of drama, human character and conflict, all the things that go to make up story-telling. The writer is blessed with a wonderful gift—the ability to enter a new world of people unlike

[ x ]

any he has ever known, to bring to them an active sympathy, the out-growth of his own past experience, to enter into their lives with understanding and to write of them *as if he were one of themselves.* Marjorie Kinnan Rawlings says in her *The Golden Apples:*

> "There are worlds within worlds. It seemed to him a shocking thing that no man could see beyond the rim of his own. Perhaps there lay the ultimate wisdom, to see all life, all living, with the acute awareness one brought to one's own."

Sigrid Undset says the writer must have:

> "insatiable curiosity toward other people's thoughts and toward horizons of undiscovered knowledge, the urge to identify oneself with others by imagination, until we suffer the sufferings of others and rejoice in their joys. These are the sources that feed our ideas about human solidarity, justice and pity and love and good-neighborliness."

We need to know our country better. We need to know not only our own region, where our roots are firmly put down, but other regions where live people different from ourselves—people of different races, faiths, cultures and backgrounds. We need to know native as well as foreign-born groups. I dislike the terms "minority groups" and "underprivileged peoples," because they imply superiority and condescension on the part of the person who uses them. When we know them, understand how they live and why, we will think of them as "people"—human beings like ourselves. When we know them, we can say: "This is the way these people live. Because I understand it, I admire and love them." Even though they haven't bathtubs and electric washers, there is a great deal to admire and love. Often people who are very poor in worldly goods have great richness of spirit.

I have wished for an invisible cloak to wear, or at least a disguise to put on when I have gone visiting the Cajuns of Louisiana or the

Crackers of Florida, so that I might be *one of them* and be accepted as such. But even then, my speech and actions would betray me. It was very inconvenient, when gathering story material in the Deep South, to look so much like a Dam-Yankee! But no—there was no other way. I had to go as myself—as an "outsider."

In the Cajun country, you are an "American"; in the Cracker country, you are a "Yankee"; in the mountains of North Carolina, you are a "foreigner" or "from the outland"; and this is always a handicap. It is difficult for any "outsider" to be accepted and to share the deeper side of their lives. The surface, yes. They are all kind and curious and very human. But there is a barrier beyond which the outsider can rarely go—until he breaks it down.

A young Louisiana librarian, in advising me, said: "Well, if I wanted to get inside the Cajun homes, I'd go out and sell them something." Strangely enough, although I wore no disguise, the children along the Louisiana bayous *did* ask me if I were selling something, because in one hand I carried a mysterious bag (containing lunch, purse, sketch book, notebooks and camera) and in the other a camp-stool, which no artist can ever travel without. Always a crowd of children gathered, eager to watch a drawing grow on a sheet of paper—and eager to tell me what I wanted to know. The children accepted me without question. Anyone who can draw pictures becomes their immediate friend. And knowing the children is but a step toward knowing the adults. Soon their mothers were asking me to come and sit on the front porch, or to come in the kitchen and have a cup of coffee. When you are invited to have coffee in Louisiana, you are no longer an "outsider."

I shall never forget an afternoon which I spent on a bayou bench, listening to an old French woman as she told me many incidents of her childhood and of three major floods through which she had lived. Equally vivid is a morning spent in the Farmer's Market of a Florida

[ xii ]

town, sitting on an upturned orange crate behind the counter, listening while Old Man Dunnaway sang *Jaybird Sittin' on a Swingin' Limb* and other folk-songs to me. When I bade him goodbye, before returning North, he grasped my hand in both his own and said: "I shall recollect you . . . in all pleasantness . . ."

From my first day in the Blue Ridge Mountains, when I hitch-hiked for six miles on a rough country road, sitting on top of a pile of feed sacks in the back of a farmer's horse-drawn wagon, on my way to visit a blind chairmaker and store-keeper, to the last day when I crossed Stone Mountain by train in a spring freshet, I met nothing but kindness. I have never known a friendlier or more truly hospitable people. You are always asked to stay for the next meal ("We haven't much, but what we have you're plumb welcome to!") or to spend the night. One mountain woman begged me to spend the summer with her ("I can't talk to nobody else the way I can talk to you.") and cried when I went away.

I met a mountain woman on the street of a country town. She was searching for a cast-iron frying pan, and when she found it the price was too high for her purse. So I offered to pay for it. After some hesitation, she accepted the gift. When I left her, she said: "I don't know who you are, but you are a good woman. Come and see me and I'll fry some chicken and give you all you can eat!"

And so, over and over again, I learned that fundamental lesson in living, that whatever you give comes back to you a hundred times over.

It is easy to see why a certain environment makes people live as they do, and affects every phase of their life—why in water-soaked Louisiana where it is too wet to raise land crops, the people make a living by fishing; and how in the dry sandy soil of Florida, a struggle is necessary to grow oranges and strawberries; and how farming on the steep hillsides in the mountains has kept the mountain people

cut off from the rest of the world. When we understand their environment and see how their lives have been conditioned thereby, then we
can understand their behavior. We can imagine ourselves in the same
situation, and we wonder if we would be different.

My own experience in getting stories from people who have lived
them has been so rich that I have tried to pass them on to others. It
is my hope that young people, reading my regional books, will share
the life of these people as I shared it, and—living it vicariously,
through the means of a vivid, dramatic, authentic, real-life story—
will learn something of that tolerance which will make all men
brothers.

I am trying to say to children that all people are flesh and blood
and have feelings like themselves, no matter where they live or how
simply they live or how little they have; that man's material comforts
should not be the end and object of life. I am trying to point out
that people of character, people who are guided by spiritual values,
come often from simple surroundings, and are worthy of our ad-
miration and even our emulation.

Just as recent American painters no longer go to Paris for painting
material, but have found here, on our own doorstep, a vivid, dramatic
America which they are portraying not romantically and senti-
mentally, but realistically and truthfully, just so accurate regional
books for children should present all the vividness and drama that
the American scene holds. We need not manufacture excitement—
it is here, inherent in the scene itself. The way that Americans have
struggled and fought and mastered their environment, in all its great
variety, is an unending American saga.

We have as many different kinds of American speech as we have
regions. It is interesting to consider in how many different ways the
American language is used. Speech is so much more than words—it
is *poetry, beauty, character, emotion.* To give the flavor of a region,

~~~~~~~~~~~~~~~~~~~~~~~~~~~~~~~~~~~~~~~~~~~~~~~~~~~~~~~~~~

to suggest the moods of the people, the atmosphere of the place, speech cannot be overlooked. When I remember the soft, velvety tones of the bayou-French people, the way they transfer our English words into their native French rhythm, when I hear again the soft, lazy drawl of the Florida Crackers, or the mountain people with fine old forgotten Elizabethan phrases on their lips, it seems to me sacrilege to transfer their speech to correct, grammatical, School-Reader English, made easy enough for the dullest child to read. To me, this would be a travesty on all the beauty and character in the lives of these people.

Words become alive only with use. A coat takes on the character of a man, after he has worn it and shaped it to his person—it becomes truly his and reflects his personality. Until words are used they are dead and lifeless. Through use, words become *living speech,* echoing the spirit within. Words need to be "worn" to attain beauty.

The sound of a horse's hoofs pounding on a country road makes a beautiful and a satisfying rhythm. The noises of nature—the cry of the crow as it flies over the field, the buzz of the bee, the hum of the locust . . . all these have their rhythm. And so does the speech of the human being. In New England, we hear one rhythm, in Louisiana another, in Florida and the mountains another. In the simplest words, with a minimum of distortions in spelling, this is what I have tried to convey. There may be some children who will find it difficult reading. But I am willing to make that sacrifice, because of all that those who *do* read will gain, in the way of understanding the "feel" of a different people, and the "flavor" of a life different from their own.

If these books should help only a few children to "see beyond the rim of their own world" and gain that "ultimate wisdom," I shall be rewarded.

\*    \*    \*

~~~~~~~~~~~~~~~~~~~~~~~~~~~~~~~~~~~~~~~~~~~~~~~~~~~~~

The material for *Blue Ridge Billy* was gathered largely in Ashe County, North Carolina, which touches Virginia on the north and Tennessee on the west. I have not, however, adhered too closely to any definite locality, choosing rather to present a more typical picture of farm life in the Blue Ridge Mountains before the coming of the automobile. All my characters are imaginary, but the incidents used were told me by people who had experienced them. I wish to thank the many friends I made in Ashe County, who advised and helped me in so many ways.

The songs, *The Two Brothers* ("Monday morning go to school"), *The Farmyard* ("Had me a cat and the cat pleased me"), *The Wife Wrapt in Wether's Skin* ("There was an old man he had a wife"), *Betty Anne* or *Pretty Little Miss* ("Oh, fly around, my pretty little miss") are taken from *English Folk Songs from the Southern Appalachians,* collected by Olive Dame Campbell and Cecil J. Sharp, and are quoted by permission of the publishers, Oxford University Press, London. The song *Ground Hog* and some verses of *Go Tell Aunt Patsy* are used by permission of Richard Chase, taken from his *Old Songs and Singing Games,* University of North Carolina Press. Other songs quoted have been taken down from the singing of individuals in the region.

For the background of handicrafts in the mountains, I have consulted *Handicrafts of the Southern Highlands* by Allen H. Eaton; for general background, *Our Southern Highlanders* by Horace Kephart; Tennessee and North Carolina WPA Guide Books, and other volumes.

*Lois Lenski*

Dunedin, Florida
*March 1, 1946*

BLUE RIDGE BILLY

*You gotta walk that lonesome valley,*
*You gotta walk it all alone;*
*Ain't nobody gonna walk it for ye,*
*You gotta walk it all by yourself. . . .*

## CHAPTER I

## *The Half-Way-Up House*

J UST in time!" said the boy.

He pushed aside a laurel bush, climbed the fence and sat down on the top rail. He took a deep breath and looked around.

Mountains were piled up like puddings before him. Some were deeply wooded; others, like patchwork quilts, were covered with fenced-in fields of green grass or plowed red soil. Beyond, a range of higher mountains loomed up. Three peaks in a row, called the Three Top range, stood out clearly on the left. To the right, higher than the others, rose "the Peak," like a sharp finger, pointing to the sky.

The sun was setting. It threw a rosy glow over the mountains, that soft radiance which comes only between sundown and dark. A few birds chirped, and from the distance, back up the steep mountain behind him, came the faint sound of chopping. Otherwise, everything was still. It was so still, the whole earth seemed to be wrapped in silence.

The boy, Billy Honeycutt, watched the rosy glow turn to purple, then to deep blue. He watched the mountains fade away in blue haze.

"Hit's a comin' on toward dark," he said to himself, still sitting motionless.

He felt a deep content, as if he had just drained to the bottom a gourdful of water, ice-cold from the spring; or, better still, as if he had just finished off a large slice of his mother's dried-apple pie, with sugar and cream on top. But no—his satisfaction was deeper than mere appetite. Why else did he hurry so to get his chores done each evening, and scramble up the mountainside? Just to watch the sun go down each night made the whole day seem easier.

He mustn't let Pappy catch him, sitting on the fence, doing nothing. He mustn't let Pappy know. Pappy would get riled, or worse still, laugh at him and joke about it. But Mammy— she would understand. Only he was too shy to talk to her. But she understood things without being told. She knew why he was always so restless and couldn't sit still in the house. She sensed his desire to roam and encouraged it.

A deeper blue filled the sky, above the sharp-pointed finger of "the Peak." Soon dusk like a heavy curtain would fall. He was glad no one—not a single soul—knew how he loved to

[ 2 ]

come here, night after night, to watch the sun go down.

Then he heard voices in the stillness.

He jumped quickly from his perch and turned back to look. He was annoyed that anyone should have found out his secret watching place.

They were women's voices. He might as well see who it was.

He left the fence and strolled back up through the woodsy mountainside. Suddenly he saw them, up beyond, through the trees. It was old Granny Trivett and her granddaughter, Sarey Sue. They were always around somewhere.

"Hoo-oo-hoo!" he called.

"Hoo-hoo!" came Sarey Sue's reply, like an echo.

Billy saw they had a sled-load of wood. It was a small mountain sled, made to carry loads over grades too steep or rough for wagons, and was used more in summer than in winter. It was pulled by Granny's cow. They had been chopping light limbs for firewood and were hauling it home. Sarey Sue held the saplings in place, while Granny whacked the cow with a long hickory stick.

"Go 'long, Old Brindle. Go 'long!" said Granny.

Granny Trivett was thin and small, with a brown, wrinkled face and sharp, dark eyes. A red head-handkerchief was tied under her chin. Her skirt of brown linsey hung long and full to her ankles, covered in front with a blue cotton-check apron.

Sarey Sue, the girl, twelve years old, was long, skinny and brown. Her brown hair hung loose and uncombed on her

[3]

shoulders. Her feet were bare beneath her linsey skirt. The evening air was chilly, but she wore no wrap.

"Here, let me help," said Billy.

Part of the load was about to fall, as the sled curved and swayed up the hill behind the slow-moving cow. Billy shoved the wood higher and shifted its weight to the center of the sled.

"I'll walk behind and ketch it, if it falls again," he said.

Sarey Sue laughed. "Don't let hit fall and bust your head!"

The cow wound slowly in and out among the trees, her bell clanging sharply.

"Hit ain't much further now," said Granny.

"Here we air," said Sarey Sue, after a little.

"At the Half-Way-Up House!" added Billy. "I always say your house is just half-way up the mountain— a good place to stop and ketch your breath."

"Law, yes," laughed Sarey Sue. "Hit shore is."

[5]

In the falling darkness, the tiny cabin seemed to be leaning against the great mountain, as if for warmth, shelter and comfort. It was built of logs, with a mud-daubed rock chimney at one end and a porch across the front. The roof was covered with hand-riven shingles or clapboards, curling loosely from age.

Sarey Sue ran in and lighted a lamp on the table beside the small window. Its feeble rays threw a slant of light across the uneven boards of the porch floor, and down the rickety steps.

Billy helped Granny unload the wood and put the cow in the shed. "I got to be goin'," he said.

"Come in, have a chair and rest yourself a while," said Granny.

"Well, I just believe I will," said Billy.

He stepped on the porch and began to sniff. The air was filled with fragrance—the pungent sweetness of sassafras, the sharp tang of various mints, the cleanness of pine bark. Great piles of roots and bark lay on the floor in dark corners of the cabin room. From the ceiling hung bunches of leaves and branches of various wildflowers and herbs. Billy sniffed again. The smell of all these wild things was satisfying.

[ 6 ]

The room was simply furnished with a bureau, a table and two split-bottom chairs. A spool bed stood in one corner, covered with a patchwork quilt, and a hand-hewed loom and wooden chest in the other. The fireplace, used for cooking, was at the end.

"Been yarbin' lately?" asked Billy, using the usual mountain expression for "gathering herbs."

"Law, yes, we been out all evenin'," said Sarey Sue. She poked at the backlog in the fireplace, then threw some small sticks of wood in front of it.

"Where'd you go? Back up on Laurel Mountain?"

"Law, no," said Granny, "over to the Peak. There was some certain roots there I'd a mind to get."

"Why that's a fur piece!" exclaimed the boy. "Must be nigh five miles, ain't hit? You-all must be tired in your bones."

"I don't never get tired," said Granny. "Or else, maybe hit's the smell o' yarbs gives me strength."

Sarey Sue sat down on a small overturned keg on the hearth, picked up a curious-looking instrument, and pushed it back and forth. Strange sounds began to come out of it, making a tune.

"We'll have us a music party!" announced the girl, leaning back and pumping vigorously.

Billy Honeycutt stared. "What's that ere thing?" he stammered.

"Hit's an accordion," answered Sarey Sue. "My Pappy had it afore he died."

[7]

"I been a-wantin' to sell hit," said Granny. "Hit's worth a sight o' money. But Sarey Sue won't hear to it. Her Pappy had that instru-ment and she's a mind to keep hit. That's *Sourwood Mountain* she's playin':

> "Chickens a-crowin' on Sourwood Mountain,
> Hay diddy ump diddy iddy um day;
> So many pretty girls I can't count 'em,
> Hay diddy ump diddy iddy um day.
> My true love is a sun-burnt daisy,
> She won't work and I'm too lazy . . ."

Sarey Sue's merry music filled the room. Then she stopped pumping and the tune was ended.

"How'd you learn to play?" asked Billy.

"Just by ear," said Sarey Sue. "I was nigh six years old when I just took it up and begun to play."

"She'd sit as unconcerned," added Granny, "and work at it as if her life depended on it, while folks stood around and laughed at her. How her Pappy laughed! Now she don't never think what she's doin'. She just rattles away on them little ole tunes, and we never get lonesome no more."

"Nobody's lonesome round here," said Sarey Sue, pumping again.

Billy sat still and watched her. His ears feasted on her tunes.

Everybody called the Trivetts poor. But they had an instrument that made music, to keep them from getting lonesome, way up here on the side of the mountain. It made finer

[ 8 ]

music than Walt Moseley's guitar, finer even—no, almost as fine—as Uncle Jamie's fiddle. No, Granny and Sarey Sue weren't poor. They were rich indeed. They could have music whenever they wanted it.

"We never have no music frolics to our house," said Billy. His voice was sad. "My Pappy don't like tune-singin'—only hymns at the church-house. We ain't got no instru-ment at all, no guitar nor banjo." He pronounced the words *git'-tar* and *ban-jer.*

"Your Mammy sang when she was young," said Granny. "All them Bronsons could sing. And your Uncle Jamie, her brother, he still sings. Why, he's called Fiddlin' Jamie, the Singin' Fiddler, all over the county."

"Law, yes, they all sing at Uncle Jamie's house," said Billy, "all the boys, Rick, Glen and Jack. And so does Ettie Bell." He paused, staring at Sarey Sue's accordion.

"I wisht I could get me an instru-ment . . ." He breathed the words softly—he scarcely dared say them. "A banjo to pick . . ." It was like wishing for the moon.

"Sarey Sue's Pappy made hisself a banjo once," said Granny brightly, "when he was just a little rabbity feller like you. He stretched a tanned groundhog skin over a cheese hoop, and shaped a stick of wood for the banjo's neck. He put bees-wax on sewin' thread for the strings."

"You might could get some horse hair from your Old Dandy's tail, for the strings," said Sarey Sue.

Billy shook his head. "Sounds like a heap o' work to me."

[9]

"You might could grub yarbs—sassyfrack or gen-sang—and earn money and get you a store-bought one," said Sarey Sue hopefully.

"Huh! You grub the whole endurin' day, gatherin' stuff like that, and get maybe a penny a pound, or two or three cents or somethin'. I'd be a little ole man afore I'd get me a banjo."

"Hit's hard work, grubbin' yarbs," admitted Granny. "If hit wasn't for that ole cow-brute and the milk and butter she gives us, and them chickens, we couldn't make out to live. The roots and yarbs just bring in a little extry. Poor people has a time in this world. I reckon they'll fare better in the next."

"Don't you get nothin' for goin' around and takin' your yarb tea and makin' ailin' folkses well?" asked Billy. "Somebody's always callin' on you to doctor 'em."

"Not money," said Granny. "The Lord give all the roots and yarbs for folkses to use, so I couldn't take no money for 'em. Sometimes somebody brings me a ham or somethin'. Last summer when Saphronia Lyle like to died, and I saved her, she brung me a goose. I been storin' the pickin's away till I git enough for a feather bed."

"Then we'll sleep in feathers," said Sarey Sue, "not on shucks no more."

But Billy was not thinking about feather beds.

"Won't you come grub sassyfrack with us?" asked Sarey Sue.

The boy shook his head. "Too much work to do at home."

"Law sakes," laughed Granny. "There's always a way round the mountain, if you can't climb over. You don't need no instru-ment to make music with, as long as you got a tongue in your head. Why don't you sing?"

"Songs ain't no good except to set and listen to," said Billy. He dropped his head shyly. "Don't know ary tunes to sing."

"You, Billy Honeycutt, don't know no tunes? Why, every boy that's worth a cent can sing. Ain't you 'shamed of your-self, when all your kinfolks been singin' from morn till night? You don't know *Cacklin' Hen?*" The next minute Granny was singing:

"Old hen cackles,
  She cackles in the barn;
  Old hen cackles,
  She cackles in the barn!
  Why she make such a hollerin' in the barn?

Old hen cackles,
  She cackles in the lot;
  Old hen cackles,
  She cackles in the lot!
  Next time she cackles, she'll cackle in the pot!"

"My Pappy used to sing that!" cried Sarey Sue, clapping her hands.

When they stopped laughing, the room grew quiet again. Granny leaned back in her oak-split rocker and began to hum softly to herself. Was she going to sing a ballad-song, one of those weird, high-pitched tunes of hers?

Billy's mother had told him that Granny's head was full of the old songs she remembered from her grandmother's and great-grandmother's singing. Granny was like all those old people who had gone on before—she could sing and sing. She knew all seventeen verses of *Barbary Allen.* But she only sang when she felt like singing. Sometimes she wouldn't sing at all. When you asked her to, she never would.

The boy sat very still, looking at the floor.

Then the sad, mournful tune began to fill the room. It was the ballad of *The Two Brothers.* Sarey Sue set her accordion on the floor, cupped her chin in her hands and listened. Billy closed his eyes dreamily. The words were soft but plain to hear. A little later, Billy made his way down the dark mountain with the tune ringing in his ears:

"Monday morning go to school,
Friday evening home;
Brother, comb my sweetheart's hair
As we go walking home.

Brother, won't you play a game of ball?
Brother, won't you toss a stone?
Brother, won't you play no other game
As we go marching home?

I can't play no game of ball,
I can't toss no stone,
I can't play no other game,
Brother, leave me alone . . ."

## CHAPTER II

# *A Turn of Corn*

"Whoa mule! Whoa, I say!
If somebody don't head that mule,
He's goin' to run away.

Whoa mule! Whoa, I say!
Got him hooked in the harness,
Got him hooked at last.

I see my mule a-comin'
He's comin' with a smile;
If you don't watch out
He'll kick you half a mile!"

BILLY HONEYCUTT'S voice rang out loud and clear through the quiet valley. He leaned against the sacks of corn and jerked the reins. His mule, Old Bet, picked her steps carefully.

The road, a rough wagon track, was filled with muddy ruts. It had rained hard for several days, and heavy wagons loaded with timber, bound for Mountain City, had left deep tracks. Winding in and about, the road followed Roundabout Creek. In two miles, it crossed the creek twenty-seven times—or, was it the creek crossing the road? Billy sometimes wondered. Usually, in dry weather, he rode on the fine gravel in the creek bed, but today the creek was full of water. A heavy rain always filled the creek up. Old Bet did not like splashing through it so many times, but Billy did.

Soon he reached the village of Solitude.

The creek turned in a wide curve to the left behind Jeb Dotson's store. Part of it ran under the store. At the left rear corner, the building had a wooden leg, which rested on a rock in the creek bed.

"Golly!" exclaimed Billy, pulling up his mule and staring in at the rear window. "Ketch me sleepin' in that ere bed with the water risin' and all!" For Jeb, a bachelor, lived in his store, and his bed, as any one could see from the window, was right in the corner, with the creek running under.

"Jeb'll git washed away some night," said Billy, and rode along.

The creek flowed on for a short distance to the dam, where it widened into a broad millpond. From one side, a narrow race carried the water along the side of the hill to a point above Hamby's mill. Billy jogged down the road, past Jasper

Jackson's big house and the church-house, till he came to the
post office, where he pulled up. The post office was probably
the smallest in the United States. It was not more than eight
feet square, with a partition through the middle, and a tiny
stove in the outer half.

"Howdy, Miss Viney. Ary letter for me?" he called.

The postmistress, who had a long nose but a genial smile,
put her head out of the little window in the partition and
shook it. "Who'd be a-writin' to you, Billy Honeycutt?"

"Dunno," said the boy. Like many mountain people, he
believed that post offices were meant to produce letters, and
he always lived in hope. "Giddap!" he called. He slapped
Old Bet and started on again.

Soon, walking in the road ahead, he saw the familiar figure

of Sarey Sue Trivett. Her small face was enclosed in a huge slat sunbonnet, and she carried a sack of corn slung across one shoulder.

"Howdy, Sarey Sue," said Billy, as he came up to her. "Walkin' to mill?"

"I reckon," answered the girl with a grin.

"Where's your mule?" inquired Billy.

"Hain't got none, less'n I borry your'n." She shifted the sack to her other shoulder.

Billy reached the mill first. He tied the little gray mule to the hitching rail, beside a brown-and-white-spotted horse already there.

The great mill-wheel stood still, but a steady trickle of water, escaping from the mossy race, dripped noisily onto the rocks below. Old Hamby sat humped over on a chair outside the door, napping. Under his dark felt hat, his long beard gleamed white. Startled from his doze by the sound of footsteps, the old man rose, picked up his stick, and looked to see who was coming.

Suddenly a loud squealing of hogs rang out. It could be heard plainly above the steady dripping of the water.

"Hogs fightin'," said Billy. "Some hogs is just mean and ornery."

Old Hamby looked back up behind the mill to the field where his barn and hog-pen were. Then he turned to the boy with eyes which gleamed piercing and black under his bushy brows.

"No, son," he said. "They're not fightin'. That just means there's gonna be a bad spell o' weather. A sow can see the wind and tell when the weather's fixin' to change."

The old man scanned the sky. Billy looked too, and saw heavy, dark clouds rolling up. A strong wind shook the tree tops.

" 'A sow can see the wind?' " he asked, in amazement. " 'A sow can . . .' what did you say, Granpap?"

But the old man had turned his back and entered the mill. Billy followed him into the dusky interior. Sacks and barrels of grain stood along the wall. Everything in the mill, the plat-form, the hopper, the stairway to the loft, was covered with white dust.

Old Hamby dumped Billy's shelled corn into the hopper and turned the lever, but nothing happened. The miller waited and looked around. Then he frowned and swore.

"What's the matter, Granpap?" asked Billy.

"Danged if I know!" answered Hamby.

"Mill's broke," said Billy to Sarey Sue Trivett, as she came in. The girl dropped her sack and pushed her bonnet back.

"Who said mill's broke?" shouted the old man angrily.

Sarey Sue and Billy stood by the door and waited. First a hen, then a rooster walked boldly in, looking for stray grains of corn. Old Hamby's cat rose from its bed on a pile of sacks and walked out. Sarey Sue kicked it idly with her bare foot.

[ 19 ]

Then, suddenly, a pig ran squealing past the open door, with a boy behind it.

"Did you know a sow can see the wind?" asked Billy. But Sarey Sue did not hear.

She and Old Hamby hustled out the door. Billy went too. He forgot his question when he saw Burl Moseley chasing the pig and beating it with a stout stick. Burl Moseley was the son of Walt Moseley, who lived in Buckwheat Hollow near Three Top. Billy knew now that the spotted horse belonged to the Moseleys.

"You son of a gun! You blatherskite!" shouted Old Hamby. "Lay your hands offen that pig or I'll wear your pants out!"

"I'll ketch him for you," shouted Billy, giving chase.

Hamby turned to the mill again. He walked around inside, then came out. He crossed the bridge over the creek to a rise of ground beyond the wheel and stared. There, on top of the race, lay his big wooden barnyard gate. It had been taken off its hinges. No wonder the sluice-gate wouldn't lift to let the water through.

Two more hogs came running. The old man stumbled and almost fell over them.

"Who let them hogs loose?" asked Sarey Sue.

"Burl Moseley!" shouted the miller angrily. "He done it while I was dozin'. I'd like to lick the livin' lard out of him. Bouncin' fools, all them Buckwheat Holler boys, just baitin' trouble ary place they go."

"Can ye grind a little turn o' corn for my Granny?" asked

[ 20 ]

Sarey Sue.

"Not till we git that big ole barnyard gate off," said Hamby.

Billy came tearing back. "I'll lay for that feller. I wisht I'd brung my pig-sticker. I'll get me a pocket full o' rocks . . ." He stopped when he saw what the miller was looking at.

"Burl done it," explained Sarey Sue. "Hamby's firin' mad."

"He couldn't a done it by hisself," said Billy. "That barn-yard gate's too heavy."

"There's the ladder he used," said Hamby. "He had help from some other bouncin' fool."

Billy helped move the ladder and lean it against the race. He climbed up and helped lift the heavy gate down. Then he saw Burl Moseley peeping round the corner of the mill, laughing. With him was Buck Norton—also from Buckwheat Hollow. The two were enjoying their joke on the old man.

"I see you-uns," shouted Hamby. "Just wait till I ketch ye!"

But Billy did not wait. He went straight for the two boys with his fists. They met on the bridge across the creek and fell over in a mad tumble, arms, fists and legs working wildly.

Old Hamby and Sarey Sue walked past them, into the open door of the mill. The miller turned the lever, and the rushing water poured over the wheel which began to revolve, and fell in a shower in the creek below the bridge. The yells and shouts of the fighting boys were drowned in the deafening noise.

Old Hamby measured out his toll from Billy's meal, then

poured Sarey Sue's corn into the hopper. The girl stood just inside the door and watched the fight. Over and over rolled the boys, nearer and nearer to the edge of the bridge. Some boys and men came down the road from the store and stopped to watch.

"Look out!" screamed Sarey Sue once or twice. "I'm skeered, Granpap, they'll roll over in the creek and git drownded!"

"Good! Let 'em roll," answered Hamby. He came to the door, and rubbing his hands together, grinned with delight. "Little Billy Honeycutt—he's a regular wildcat, now ain't he? A chip offen the old block. I never thought he had it in him. He always looked a peaceable young feller to me."

"Not when he gits riled," said Sarey Sue, smiling back.

The rolling boys hovered on the edge of the bridge.

"O-o-o-oh!" screamed Sarey Sue, dancing on her bare toes. "I'm skeered! I'm skeered!"

If only she had a pole, she could poke them back. But she had no pole. Old Hamby came out again. "Here's your poke o' meal," he said, placing it on her shoulder.

A sudden notion seized her. She must stop the fighting before Billy Honeycutt got killed. She passed the boys quickly and ran over to the hitching rail. She heaved her sack up on Old Bet, Billy's mule, and looked back to see if the boy was watching. Sure enough, a tousled head poked itself up from the tangled, rolling mass and a voice shouted: "Hold on there, Sarey Sue! You can't take my mule. I got two pokes o' my

[ 23 ]

own to tote."

The fighters paused to draw breath, the mass wavered and became still. Three tousled heads looked in the girl's direction, which was just what she wanted.

"Then I'll take Burl's nag," answered Sarey Sue shrilly. She lifted her sack from the mule's to the horse's back. "I'm just too doggone tired to tote this heavy poke all the way up that ere mountain. What's horses fer, nohow, but to tote meal for gals?"

She untied the reins. She threw herself across the horse's back, lifted a leg and sat astride. "Well, let's go!" she called gaily. "You-all can just keep right on fightin'!"

Old Hamby and the loafing men, standing in the mill door, roared with laughter.

The fight ended abruptly.

"Hey there!" shouted the angry Burl. "Where you a-goin', gal, on my horse? Don't you dare take that horse. I ain't never said you could!" He started out on a run to follow her. "Hey there!" he screamed. "That nag's wild! She's mean and ornery. She'll throw you shore!"

But Sarey Sue was speeding up the road, well out of hearing.

It did not take Billy long to follow. He flung his sacks on Old Bet and was off up the road while Burl and Buck stood gaping.

"Burl says his horse is wild!" he called to Sarey Sue, as he came up beside her.

Sarey Sue nodded her head. Although she had no horse

of her own, she was quite at home on a horse's back. She rode
every chance she got—on other people's horses.

"I can beat anybody ridin'," she answered. "There ain't
a hoss in these mountains I can't ride. The wilder, the better."

"Ain't you never got throwed?" asked Billy.

"Once," she admitted. "Once I was ridin' Uncle Fred's nag,
when a cussed little ole dog jumped out in front and scared
her, and she throwed me smack-dab in a mud puddle."

"Did you git hurt?"

"No—just covered with mud!"

They followed the road up Roundabout Creek, loping along
easily and splashing through the fords. A flock of geese
scattered as they dashed through, and a few stray sheep pelted
blindly against the fence to get out of their way.

"Let's race!" shouted Billy, as they came to a smooth stretch.

Sarey Sue nodded. They both slapped the reins. Neck to
neck they moved along, then Burl's horse began to leave Old
Bet behind.

Billy fell back. Old Bet was a small mule, with a smooth
even gait, and Billy liked to ride her because there was no
jolting. But she couldn't keep up with Burl's horse.

"You better not beat me," called Billy. "A little ole mule
can't keep up with a big race-horse. Wait for me, Sarey
Sue . . ."

An overhanging limb from a tree close by the road nearly
brushed him off. He dodged.

"No fair—you takin' the creek side," he complained.

"Makin' me dodge all the bushes."

Sarey Sue turned, a broad smile on her face. "Hurry along! Hurry, why don't you?"

Another limb hung low, then a whole cluster of them. Billy warded off the biggest one with his arm, but it came down again with full force on his top sack of meal. The sack fell off and spilled. The sharp limb had torn a hole in the cloth. Old Bet stopped of her own accord.

"Looky here what you done, Sarey Sue," called the boy. "Looky here! You—racin' that wild hoss that don't belong to you! And Pappy told me not to tarry . . ."

But Sarey Sue did not see or hear. She and her wild horse had vanished up the creek. Billy shook his fist after her. Then he bent over to gather up the spilled meal. He tied up the

sack as best he could and started on again.

He jogged contentedly along the road, watching the creek. The water was much higher now. The "branches" that ran into it from the hillsides were babbling noisily and were white with foam. There had been a lot of rain and it was going to rain again. The sky looked dark and lowering.

Billy remembered what Old Hamby had said: *A sow can see the wind.* What color was it then? And how did the old man know? Hogs couldn't talk. And what did a sow have to do with the weather, anyway? But—a black storm was really coming. Thunder began to roll.

Billy thought again of Jeb Dotson's bed, perched so perilously close to Roundabout Creek. Why did the storekeeper build his store with one leg in the creek, when there was plenty of high land to build on? He wished he had stopped in at the store and talked to Jeb about it. But Pappy had told him not to tarry.

He slapped Old Bet and called "Giddap."

Then Jeb Dotson and his problems faded from the boy's mind, for he saw the spotted Moseley horse coming back down the road, without a rider. Had Sarey Sue reached home, unloaded her meal and sent the horse back? Or, if the horse was wild as Burl said, had it thrown her? Everybody said that if Sarey Sue Trivett didn't stop riding other people's horses, she was sure to get killed some day. What if the horse had thrown her and she was lying under a bush half dead?

The Moseley horse began to nibble grass by the fence. She

was quiet enough now. Billy patted her on the nose and talked to her. Then he shooed her off down the road toward the mill. She could find her way home all right, all the way to Buckwheat Hollow, if Burl was not waiting for her at the mill.

Billy rode on until he came to a fork. Straight ahead, following the creek, the road led to his own home in Hoot Owl Hollow. To the right, a narrow trail ran up the mountainside to the Half-Way-Up House where the Trivetts lived.

Billy hesitated. Should he ride up and see what had happened to Sarey Sue? Or, should he go on home where Pappy would be waiting?

A loud peal of thunder answered the question. The rain began to come down in torrents.

"Golly! The meal's gettin' wet," said Billy. He raised his hand to his left eye and was surprised to find it badly swollen.

"What'll Pap say—me late, and a black eye! He'll know I fit!"

CHAPTER III

## Spring Freshet

G O FILL the tubs and washpot, Billy," said Mrs. Honeycutt.
"Aw, hit's too wet to wash clothes today," grumbled
the boy. "Golly! What a cloudburst that was! Mighty near
washed our house away, didn't it?"

"Nothin' but a spring freshet," said Mammy, unconcerned.

Breakfast was over, and Billy, bruised and sore from his
fight the day before, did not feel like carrying innumerable
buckets of water.

"Cloudburst or not, I'm washin' today," said his mother.
"Time we git the clothes hung up, the sun'll be over the
mountain. Your Pappy said you should help, afore he went
off this morning. When he seen your black eye, he said he
wouldn't thrash ye, but just *work* ye, this time. That'll learn

you to stay away from them Buckwheat Holler boys."

"Where's Pappy gone, Mammy?" asked Billy.

"Yonder, up Laurel Mountain, to see about them logs," said Mrs. Honeycutt, "and slide 'em down the holler. After that big rain, them old logs sure will slide in the mud."

"Wisht I could watch 'em," said Billy. "After a cloudburst they'll shore go hell-a-kitin' or faster."

"Well, you can't. Go git that water like I told ye."

Billy took the cedar buckets and went out the back door. The two little redheads followed at his heels—Mazie, the "least un," three, and Red Top, five, whose real name was Rudolphus, like his father's.

Billy turned on them. "Stop taggin' after me," he said. "Go back in the house and behave yourselves. Skedaddle quick!" They ran.

He set the buckets down, stood for a moment and stretched. If only he could stretch all the soreness out of his bones and muscles. That was the worst thing about a fight—you didn't feel it while you were fighting, but you felt it for such a long time afterwards.

The rain was over and the skies were blue again. Billy looked around in surprise. The weather changes in the mountains were so sudden. He remembered how hard it had poured all night, and how the lightning flashed and the thunder roared. He'd been wakened by trees banging on the roof and doors and windows rattling. A cloudburst, Pap said. It was hard to believe it could end so soon.

[ 30 ]

But the creek—Roundabout Creek must be high. It had been high for several days and must have risen even higher in the night. He ran down to see.

The Honeycutt house sat on a level plain in the valley of the Roundabout, in what was called Hoot Owl Hollow. The valley was hemmed in on both sides by steep hills which were really young mountains. On the far side, the wooded hill rose up thick and impenetrable from the creek below. On the near side, behind the house with its narrow fore yard, behind the few farm buildings and the fenced-in lots for garden, chicken yard, hog-pen and cow-yard, the Honeycutt farm of cultivated fields and woods rose steeply up to meet the sky.

The house had front and back porches, hand-riven shingles on the roof and a large rock chimney at the end, like most other mountain homes. The front porch had a "plunder room" for storage at one end.

Billy ran down to the creek. Both its banks had overflowed.

"Golly!" he said, as he stared. "I never seen Old Roundabout so high before." Suddenly he screamed out: "Mammy! Mammy!"

His mother put her head out the open front door.

"Mammy! Looky how high the creek is," the boy called.

"What you yellin' for, like somebody's been drownded?" answered his mother. "Go fill them buckets like I told ye, and get that fire a-goin' under the washpot." She disappeared from sight.

"Jumpin' crickets!" exclaimed Billy. "Old Roundabout's

shore on a rampage."

He ran to the ford, the widest, shallowest place in the stream, where Pappy always drove his wagon across to the road. It was waist-high in water.

"I bet hit's over the top of the wagon wheels," said Billy. "Little Old Bet couldn't walk through that, without gittin' washed off her feet and carried right down with the current."

Then he saw the footlog. It rested on piles of rocks, to keep it high off the water. There were steps up and down at the ends. The water was lapping the under side of the log. Who'd want to walk over it now?

"Golly!" said Billy to himself. "Even *I'd* be skeered."

Logs and loose brush, sticks and rails from fences were being carried downstream. Pieces of short firewood from somebody's woodpile went sailing by. A hencoop with a live rooster riding on top came along. Billy poked at it with a stick, wading deep in the water. He tried to bring it to shore, but it went floating on. Then he remembered Jeb Dotson's bed.

He looked at the footlog again. How could anybody get to the store? He tore madly into the house.

"Mammy, I got to go to the store. I got to go right off, quick!" he cried excitedly.

"You got to go fill that washpot and start that fire," said his mother. She was a small, plump woman, and wore her hair drawn back in a knot on top of her head. She was young, but already wrinkles were showing in her good-natured face. She set her lips in a firm line.

"Your Pap said I should work you hard today. What do you want to go to the store for? I ain't said I need anything." She sounded cranky.

"Just want to see Jeb Dotson," mumbled Billy.

He turned to his sister, who was fifteen and nearly grown up.

"Letty Jo," he whispered, "can't you spill the sody or hide the coffee, so I'll have to get some more at the store?"

"I know what you want," Letty Jo answered. "You want to have another fight with Burl Moseley and get t'other eye blacked up to match." She laughed.

"No, I want to . . ."

But it was no use. He knew he could not go to Solitude again today, after staying so long the day before. Slowly he

[ 33 ]

went out the back door and picked up the wooden buckets.

"Fetch me that jar o' buttermilk from the spring-house, son," his mother called after him.

It was cold inside the spring-house. Water from the spring flowed over the flat rocks where the milk crocks sat. Outside the door, the water poured from a pipe into a banked-up pool, which overflowed into the "branch." Billy picked up the gourd dipper and took a drink—the water was always ice-cold. He carried the buttermilk to the house and came back. He dipped the buckets and filled them.

The "branch" was high and its banks had overflowed. Under a tree on a rise of land, the washtubs sat on a bench. Not far off, the black iron washpot rested on three rocks over a bed of wet ashes. Billy carried a good many buckets of water to fill the pot, crossing back and forth over the shaky plank.

Letty Jo came out of the house with a basket of soiled clothes, the two little ones tagging behind her.

"Drink o' water," said Mazie.

"Drink o' water," echoed Red Top.

They started over the plank, but Billy stopped them just in time. The water suddenly carried the plank off down the branch.

"Go back to the house," ordered Billy, "afore you fall in the branch and drownd yourselves."

They ran to the back steps and sat down.

"Did you hide the coffee, Letty Jo?" Billy asked. "Did you tell Mammy she's outa coffee and needs some more?"

Letty Jo tossed her head. "You can't play no such tricks as that, just to get to the store."

Billy brought some dead chestnut wood, shaved off some kindling with his knife and started the fire. He brought an armful of larger wood and stayed only long enough to see the flames burning. Then he disappeared around the front of the house, where he waited. He waited until he saw, by peeping round the corner, that the washing was well under way. Mammy was rubbing clothes at the tub, Letty Jo had a long stick and was punching down the clothes in the wash-pot to keep them from boiling over. Mazie and Red Top were making mud pies in the wet mud beside the branch.

Billy decided it was safe to go. They were all so busy, they would never miss him. He hurried to the footlog.

He stood and looked at it. It was wet and slippery. The angry creek water was touching its under side, ready to lift it off its foundations and carry it downstream. The railing was gone. Billy himself had torn off some of its supports and broken them up for kindling. There was nothing to hold onto.

The boy looked from the footlog to the ford. He could wade through the ford and get soaked to the skin, or he could cross over the footlog and stay dry—maybe. He decided to try to stay dry. He took two steps on the log.

He had never liked the footlog much. When he was six,

and first started to school, and had to cross it every day in the wintertime, Mammy always told him not to look down at the water. But he always did, and then he got scared and dropped his dinner bucket. He had to take time to fish it out of the creek with a long stick, and that made him late and his "school biscuits" were wet for his dinner.

But now, all he had to do was to watch each step. He took a third and a fourth. He looked down at the water. He wasn't afraid of low water any more, but when it was high like today . . . "Golly!" he exclaimed, and flopped down on the log and held on tight. Then he began to crawl.

When he was halfway over, he slipped, and reaching out to grab the limb of an overhanging tree, nearly fell in. Just then, an uprooted tree came crashing down and slid under the footlog.

"Gosh-almighty!" whispered Billy in a frightened voice. "That was a close shave!"

He got over safely. His hands and feet were wet—that was all.

Then he tore down the road as fast as he could go. It was a long way to Solitude without a mule to ride. But he had to get to the store.

It was long past dinnertime when he returned.

This time he ran across the footlog, balancing himself with his two arms outstretched. It wasn't so scary now. The water had gone down more than a foot.

The washing was done—he was glad of that. He could tell because all the clothes were hanging on the rope line on the front porch and across the boards that served for a railing. He thought it wise to circle the house and come in by the open back door.

"Danged if I ain't hungry!" he said to himself. "I come nigh forgettin' all about dinner."

He lifted the cloth on the kitchen table, but there was nothing there—only the sugar bowl and spoon holder. Dinner had been eaten and everything washed up and put away. Hadn't they even missed him?

Then he heard voices in the front room. Who could it be? He slid in as quietly as he could.

There was Old Man Pozy sitting comfortably by the fireplace. There sat Mammy with her quilt patches on her lap and Letty Jo with her knitting. And at Uncle Pozy's feet, Mazie and Red Top were building a house out of corncobs. Over by the door was a large pile of Uncle Pozy's baskets.

Billy almost wished he hadn't gone away. His feet were soaked and he was chilled through. He shivered.

Uncle Pozy was talking. He was a good storyteller. He was telling about a bear hunt: "The man sot stock still on the end of the log. The bear got tired o' waitin', picked herself up and come closer . . . and closer . . . and then . . ."

*Ker-CHEW!* Billy sneezed. "Then what happened?" The question popped out of his mouth before he knew it.

They all turned their eyes from Uncle Pozy to look at Billy, forgetting the bear story.

"What? You here?" demanded Letty Jo.

"Where you been, you disobedient rascal?" asked his mother. "I been nigh in a franzy, thinkin' you'd fell in the creek and got drownded. Where you been?"

"Just out roamin'," answered Billy, shamefaced. He sat down on a stool on the hearth and tucked his wet feet under him. The heat felt good on his back. He tried to stop shivering.

"Tell me where you been, young feller!" demanded his mother again. But her tone was not as fierce as the words sounded.

It was hard for her to be stern, Billy knew, when Uncle Pozy was there. Everybody liked Old Man Pozy, who was fat and jovial, and called him Uncle. He was no kin to the Honeycutts. He lived by himself in a cabin in Honeysuckle

[ 38 ]

Hollow, on the far side of Solitude.

"Oh, Mammy!" cried Billy. "Jeb Dotson's bed got flooded and him in it! The water rose three feet high there in his store, and hit washed that leg that stood in the creek clean off, and switched the whole store roundabout. Hit's the Roundabout Store now for sure. The front door's round on the side facin' the road. And Jeb's bedroom's restin' on that big flat rock that used to be his doorstep."

"Bless goodness!" cried Mrs. Honeycutt. "Why didn't you tell us, Uncle Pozy?"

"Hit's shore news to me," replied the old man. "I come through Solitude yesterday, Ruthie. Mind I said I spent the night at Jerushy Wilcox's? I come down the Turn-Off to get here. I figgered I could get this far nohow and maybe you'd be needin' some baskets."

"And Jeb's bed, did hit get washed away?" asked Letty Jo.

"He woke up in the night and heard water washin' and he thought he was ridin' in a boat," Billy continued. "Then he felt his feet gettin' wet, and then his cornshuck mattress, and then his pillow. By that time he was wide awake, and seen the walls bein' switched around . . ."

"Could he see in the dark?" asked Red Top. "Has he got eyes like a tabbity cat?"

Billy ignored the question. "When he got outa bed, he waded water up to his waist, till he found a match to light his lamp——"

"The lamp musta been up on the shelf, so hit kept dry,"

interrupted Letty Jo, "and the matches too."

Billy glared. "Who's tellin' this story, you or me? Well, Jeb climbed up on the counter in the store and slept the rest of the night there, as comfortable as a settin' hen on her nest."

"But you said he was all wet!" protested Letty Jo.

Billy frowned and went on: "When daylight come and he looked out, the store was all switched roundabout. He don't have to put a new leg under the corner, 'cause hit's restin' right on that big ole door stone, as solid as can be. And the door faces the road now, so wagons can back right up and dump their pokes off. Jeb says he don't need no doorstep."

"How's women-folks to get up there?" asked Mammy.

"Jump, I reckon," said Billy, "if they come afoot. But hit's just right for lightin' down from a nag."

Everybody laughed.

"And Jeb ain't got pneumony?" asked Uncle Pozy.

"Not as I noticed," said Billy. "He looked spry as a cricket to me. So many folkses come to see and hear all about the flood, he was a-doin' a roarin' trade. They say hit's the worst freshet there's been in fifty year."

"Was the water all gone down when you was there?" asked Letty Jo.

"Law, yes," said Billy. "And the floor was dry."

"Three foot high you say the water was?" asked Uncle Pozy.

"That's what Jeb said."

"Went down mighty quick, didn't hit?" said Mammy, with a faint smile on her lips.

"Hit's a 'so' tale!" said Billy crossly. "If you don't believe me, just listen to this. I seen all Jeb's beddin' hangin' out

on a rope line to dry, and his nightshirt too, at the side of the store, in the sun. And his shuck mattress was up on the roof . . ."

"But Jeb ain't got pneumony," said Mammy, smiling.

"He's fit as a fiddle!" Uncle Pozy laughed and so did the others.

Billy let them laugh. He was glad Uncle Pozy was there. Nobody scolded him for running away and staying so long.

"And oh, Mammy!" he went on, his eyes sparkling. "Jeb's got a banjo in his store that he traded for one day last week. He said there was an old man died over to Cabbage Creek and didn't leave nothin' but a banjo, and his daughter traded it to Jeb for sugar and flour. Said she couldn't eat a banjo."

"Musta been old Mack Miller's daughter," said Uncle Pozy.

"What'll she eat when the banjo's et?" asked Mammy.

Uncle Pozy began to gather his baskets together. They were of various shapes and sizes. By running a rope under their handles and draping them over his back and shoulders, he could carry quite a number.

"No need to hurry," said Mrs. Honeycutt. "Can't you tarry a while and stay to supper, Uncle Pozy? We ain't got much, but what we got you're plumb welcome to. Rudy won't like it to hear you've come and gone."

"Thank ye kindly, Ruthie," said Uncle Pozy, "but Ollie Holbrook's expectin' me. There's always welcome bread at Ollie's too."

"Spend the night with us," urged Mrs. Honeycutt, "and

get a soon start in the mornin'."

"Ollie might think I got drownded in the spring freshet, if I don't go this evenin'," said Uncle Pozy. "And he wants a half-bushel measurin' basket, so that's one I can sell."

"I wisht we might could buy one," said Mammy, "but with all the baskets we got already——"

Billy stared hard at Uncle Pozy. "Do you *sell* 'em?" he asked.

"Why, shore as shootin'," replied the old man. "What you think I make 'em for? To eat 'em for dinner?"

"You *make* 'em?" demanded Billy. "What out of?"

Suddenly a commonplace basket, the like of which he had seen every day in his life, became a thing of vital interest. The mere sight of the banjo in the store had done it. All his hunger for music had been aroused. Suddenly Billy wanted that banjo with all his heart, and the baskets suggested a way to get it.

"White-oak splits," answered Uncle Pozy. "I go in the woods and pick me out a straight oak tree and cut it down. . . ."

"Can I come help you?" asked Billy breathlessly.

"You shore can, son. I'll learn you how to make splits and weave 'em into baskets, you little whippersnapper. Wanta rive shingles, too?"

Billy shook his head. He was so excited, he could not speak. He'd earn money and buy that banjo.

Uncle Pozy went to the door.

Mrs. Honeycutt said, "Now, *come!*"

Uncle Pozy answered, "Yes, I *will*, and *you* come."

After he was gone, Mrs. Honeycutt turned to her son. "What on earth's got into you, Billy? First runnin' off, and now makin' baskets. Who wants baskets, when we got more'n we need already?"

Billy dropped his eyes. It was coming. He was going to get his licking after all. Well, he'd let Mammy whip him and get it over with before Pappy came home.

"I won't run away no more, Mammy . . ." His voice became a sorrowful whine, sure to soften Mammy's heart. Sometimes she was hard outside, but he knew she was always soft inside. And the crust was not very deep.

"MAZIE!" A terrified scream came from Letty Jo, who was looking out of the small front window.

They rushed out on the porch. From there they could see Uncle Pozy, laden down with baskets, crossing the footlog, and little Mazie tagging at his heels. In all her three years, Mazie had never crossed the footlog before, and beneath it, the water was still a raging torrent.

"Looky!" cried Letty Jo, pointing upstream. A large mass of logs, sticks and brush was floating down. Would it clear the footlog?

Billy did not wait to see. He ran on feet that scarcely touched the ground. He ran halfway across the footlog, snatched his little sister up in his arms, and bore her back again. Just then the pile of brush roared past, taking the footlog with it.

[ 44 ]

Billy shook his finger in Mazie's face. "Ain't I told you to stay in the house and behave yourself?"

Uncle Pozy was safe on the other side, walking up the road. He had not seen or heard the child coming. He turned his head only when he heard Billy's voice. He waved his hand and went on.

Letty Jo stood on the porch and cried aloud, wiping her tears on her cotton-check apron.

Mammy took Mazie in her arms and carried her into the house. She sat down in her split-oak rocker in front of the fire and hugged the child tight. Billy dropped on the floor at her feet, out of breath. She put her hand on his tousled head. Then she said gently:

"Son, you ain't had no dinner, have you?"

CHAPTER IV

## *Over the Mountain*

"Had me a cat and the cat pleased me,
  Fed my cat in yonders tree;
  The cat went fiddle-i-dee.

  Had me a dog and the dog pleased me,
  Fed my dog in yonders tree;
  The dog went boo, boo, boo,
  And the cat went fiddle-i-dee.

  Had me a hen and the hen pleased me,
  Fed my hen in yonders tree;
  The hen went ka, ka, ka,
  The dog went boo, boo, boo,
  And the cat went fiddle-i-dee.

  Had me a hog and the hog pleased me,
  Fed my hog . . ."

BILLY HONEYCUTT'S singing stopped abruptly. He was well up the side of the mountain, climbing fast. Breathless, he took hold of the limb of a tree and pulled himself up on a rock.

Down, far below he could see his father's house. Through the valley ran the road and the creek side by side. He saw Pappy's horse, Old Dandy, on the road, moving along like a tiny crawling ant. He knew the horse carried his mother and the little ones, and that Letty Jo was walking by their side. They were off to spend the day at Uncle Jamie's in Last Hope Hollow.

Uncle Jamie was his mother's brother, and Aunt Tallie was his wife. They had three boys, Rick, Glen and Jack, and one girl, Ettie Bell. Billy was fond of his cousins, but this time he did not want to go along. It was the first time he had ever refused to go.

Billy carried the dream of a banjo in the back of his head. Ever since Granny Trivett had talked about it, the dream had been there. He couldn't forget it, waking or sleeping. He could see that banjo hanging in Jeb Dotson's store. He could all but feel the strings under his fingers. Uncle Pozy's visit had made his dream almost a reality. He must get to

Uncle Pozy's. He would make baskets and trade them for the banjo. *All his life he had been without one. . . .*

[ 47 ]

That was why he refused to go to Uncle Jamie's. "I want to go roamin'," he had told Mammy.

His mother looked at him closely. "Where?" she asked.

"Up yonder on the mountain," he said. "Ain't been up there in a month o' Sundays. Dogwood'll soon be out and crabthorn too. . . ."

"Not yet awhile," said Mammy. But she let him go.

Now, as he made his steep way up again, he was glad he had come. Through the cold winter he had been cooped up in the house or in school for so long. He liked school well enough, but was glad it lasted for only two months in the winter. He always got tired of sitting, it made him so restless.

"No matter how whizzin' cold it gits," he said to himself, "I druther be outside any day."

The vision of the banjo returned. But meanwhile, he remembered what Granny Trivett had said—he had a mouth to sing with. All the mountain people liked to sing and, once he thought about it, he was surprised to find how many songs he knew. All day long, tunes kept popping into his head.

He saw some birds hopping on a limb. "Hey, chewink! Hey, chitterlink! If you-uns can sing, reckon I can too." He went on with his song:

> "Had me a calf and the calf pleased me,
> Fed my calf in yonders tree;
> The calf went ma, ma, ma,
> The cow went moo, moo, moo,
> The sheep went baa, baa, baa,

The hog went kru-si, kru-si, kru-si,
The hen went ka, ka, ka,
The dog went boo, boo, boo,
And the cat went fiddle-i-dee!"

Now he was on top of the ridge, along which ran a narrow trail. Sometimes people came up here with a land sled to bring down firewood or a load of hay from the far-off side. Looking back, he could see over Solitude, and beyond to Three Top and the Peak. Looking forward, a whole new valley opened up at his feet—Bearskin Hollow and No Man's Cove, and the long Stone Mountain range that divided North Carolina from Tennessee; and still beyond, far-off ranges lost in blue, blue haze. No wonder they were called the Blue Ridge Mountains.

Uncle Pozy lived down in Honeysuckle Hollow, and Billy was following a short-cut to get there. Around by the road through Solitude, it was seven or eight miles, but up over the ridge and down again, it was only four. Of course he might get off the trail and lose himself, and there might be bears in the laurel thickets, they were so dense. But he knew that if he went about halfway to Bearskin Creek, and then turned right instead of left, he would get there. He'd better hurry, the sun was already high. He'd be plenty hungry by dinnertime.

He started down the mountainside running. Then he slowed up suddenly, for he saw figures in the woods below. At first he thought they were not real. They looked like trees moving. Or were they animals? They seemed to be part of the pattern of branches and trees. They were not people at all. Pappy said people should always wear something bright red in the woods, so hunters wouldn't shoot them by mistake.

Only when he heard voices was he sure. He hurried on.

"Where you off to, Billy Honeycutt?"

It was Sarey Sue Trivett's thin voice. And there was her Granny beside her. They were out herbing again. Wherever you went on the mountain, they were always there. They were always taking wood and roots and bark off other people's land. Pappy said they acted as if they owned the whole mountain, but everybody knew they were too poor to own but a patch.

"Where you off to?" asked Sarey Sue again.

"Nowhere," he said briefly. "Just a-roamin'."

"What you roamin' for?" persisted Sarey Sue.

"Just to be a-roamin'."

Why did they have to know everything? The two of them looked a disreputable pair. Their ragged clothes were torn by briars and brambles. Their faces and hands were smudged.

"You look like an ole raggedy-drag," Billy said to Sarey Sue.

[ 50 ]

The girl tossed her head. "Been to mill lately?" she asked, with a grin.

He remembered he had not seen her since she rode off on Burl Moseley's horse. Sarey Sue looked perfectly whole. She did not limp or carry an arm in a sling. It would be hard to kill off Sarey Sue.

"Burl's nag didn't throw you, did she?" Billy asked.

"That sorry little ole critter?" sniffed Sarey Sue. "No, sir. Just went so slow, I thought I'd git home faster afoot, so I turned her loose."

Billy laughed. Trust Sarey Sue. Nobody's fool—Sarey Sue.

"How's your poor eye?" she asked, full of sympathy.

"What eye?" demanded Billy.

It was yellow and green now instead of black and blue, but no self-respecting boy ever admitted that a black eye *hurt*.

"Did you come to help us dig yarbs?" asked Sarey Sue, smiling. "To trade for that store-bought banjo you're hankerin' for?"

The remark stirred him deeply.

"Naw," he answered.

The banjo dream was something sacred, that lived only in the back of his head. Why did she have to talk about it out loud?

"Don't you never breathe a word to nobody about me a-cravin' a banjo!" he said angrily.

"No?" answered Sarey Sue, in surprise.

"Got a better way to earn money than grubbin' roots," he

said. "Easier too . . ." He kicked at the basket sitting on the ground at the girl's feet. "What you got in there? Nasty bunch of ole dirty weeds, eh?"

Granny Trivett, who had been digging busily and had as yet said no word, turned and looked at the boy almost fiercely.

"There ain't no such thing as a weed," was her sharp reply. "Just 'cause the good Lord made a plant to grow so plentiful hit can't never be killed out, that don't make hit a weed. He never made nary thing that ain't good for somethin'. Most 'weeds' as you call 'em, make good medicine to cure disease."

"Gran keeps her medicine pot a-simmerin' by the fire all the time," put in Sarey Sue. "Sometimes hit smells awful."

"And who do ye reckon gits all these yarbs we trade in at the store?" Granny's eyes pierced the boy through.

"Jeb Dotson," he said sullenly.

"Jeb don't do nothin' but sell 'em again. Who buys 'em from Jeb?" demanded Granny.

"Danged if I know!" answered Billy.

"Well, I'll tell ye. Jeb sells 'em to a big drug company in North Wilkesboro," said Granny, "and the drug company sends the stuff off somewheres to a factory, where hit's made up into bottle medicines and pills and powders and I don't know what-all. Off there, in them fur-off parts, they have drugstores where them furrin' doctors buy that stuff to cure folkses with. That's what that 'nasty ole bunch o' weeds' is good for. Didn't ye know that? And you been goin' to school too."

[ 52 ]

"Don't learn nothin' 'bout yarbs at school," mumbled Billy. "We read outen books."

Granny picked up her mattock and began to swing it high over her head.

"When Gran's out of snuff, hit makes her crosser'n a hornet," explained Sarey Sue. Then in a friendly tone, "I seen a rattlesnake, Billy."

"Huh! That's nothin ," grunted the boy.

"I reached down to pull a vine away from a root I was grubbin' and I jumped back like I'd been shot," Sarey Sue went on. "First I thought hit was a bull nettle, then I heard hit singin'. I called Granny and we looked for a dogwood or a sourwood tree to get a stout stick to kill hit, but we couldn't find nary a one. And the rocks was all too heavy to tote. So we picked up that poke o' bark and my basket and we come down this-a-way in a hurry. Right up there on the ridge hit was."

Granny Trivett was never one to miss the chance to tell a tale. There had been no real danger, but she had imagination enough to know what *might* have happened.

"Lordy mercy, son," she continued the girl's story, "if that snake had a struck Sarey Sue, I don't know what I'd a done. Sarey Sue's big for her age and heavy, for all she looks so spindlin'. I'd a been bound to git her out of there, but she'd a been too heavy for me to tote, and I couldn't a left her there —she'd a been dead afore I coulda brung help."

"And we couldn't run a step," added Sarey Sue, " 'twas that

rough up there—right atop the Drop-Off."

"All the snakes is comin' out o' their winter nestses now," said Billy. "I reckon the spring sunshine feels just as good to them as to us. But I hain't seen no dogwood out yet."

"I hain't neither," said Sarey Sue. "Well, talkin' hain't grubbin'. Gimme that maddick!" She took the heavy digging tool and began to swing it up and down. Her thin arms looked as if they could not lift it, but she swung it briskly, digging a deep hole beside a young tree.

"That ain't sassyfrack!" screamed Granny. "That's a hickory. Leave hit alone, gal. Don't ye go grubbin' up all the trees in the woods." She turned to the boy. "Sarey Sue thinks she knows roots and yarbs, but seems like I can't never learn her."

"She must be dumb," said Billy. "Hickory and sassyfrack don't look the same."

Sarey Sue kept right on digging, until she got a piece of the root. She brushed the dirt off, put it in her mouth and chewed it. Then she threw it down. Granny was right. It was not sassafras. "Didn't hurt the little ole tree none," she said. She dug again and pulled up another root.

"What's that?" asked Billy.

"Law me, don't you know?" asked Sarey Sue. "Stone root. Root's hard as stone, so hard you can't break it with your hands." She chopped it in two with her mattock. "There, feel of it," she said. "The inside feels cold and hard like stone."

Billy agreed. "What else you got? Thought you was just grubbin' sassyfrack."

"Little of everything," said Sarey Sue. "Crowhosh, coon root, hog-grub, poke root——"

"Never seed poke root ever git dry," interrupted Granny. "Let it lay out in the sun for days and days and hit won't dry. Don't pay to mess round with hit."

"There's lobelia," said Sarey Sue, pointing. "That'll kill ye."

"Some folkses take hit and make a syrup," said Granny. "Best thing for a cough that ever was."

"Lordy mercy, I'm skeered to drink it!" exclaimed Sarey Sue, laughing. "Blame stuff's pizen!"

"If a chicken eats one seed of it," said Granny, "hit'll drop over dead."

"Sassyfrack's the best root to grub," said Sarey Sue. "They

[ 55 ]

make them cold drinks out of it. They can't git enough of it."

"Sassyfrack tea's mighty good," said Billy.

"Wisht I had five acres of it," said Granny. "I'd clear it all out. Don't darst burn the wood, though. Hit's bad luck to burn it."

Suddenly Billy remembered Uncle Pozy and his baskets. Instead of talking to the Trivetts, he ought to be out with Uncle Pozy, choosing a white-oak tree for splits. "Well, I got to mosey on down the mountain," he said.

Before he could move, Granny Trivett leaned over and clutched the boy's arm. "Who's that a-goin' there?" she whispered.

Below them, moving above a clump of laurel, they saw a man carrying a gun on his shoulder.

"Why, hit looks like Pappy out huntin'," sail Billy, surprised. "I'll holler to him."

"No, ye won't," said Granny. "Ye just hush."

"Hit shore do look like your Pappy," said Sarey Sue.

"I hear hounds a-squealin'," said Billy. "They're after a fox."

"Not in broad daylight," said Granny in a low voice.

Billy knew that foxes were hunted in daylight, and coons and possums at night. He was big enough to fox-hunt himself, and he knew all about animals and their tracks. Granny was talking through her hat. But why?

"Let's go down where Pap is and see," said Billy.

"Law, no, you stay right here," said Granny, "and hush

[ 56 ]

your mouth. Don't talk so loud. Don't ye know folks down there in the holler can hear every word you say?"

"Let's go see what he's ketchin'——"

"Law, no," said Granny, pressing her lips firmly. "A woman mustn't never go near a man a-huntin'. Hit brings bad luck, they say."

"Then I'll go see myself," said Billy.

"You'll stay right where you be!" Granny's voice was cold and stern. Billy looked at her, astonished.

"I guess I'll go where I please. I'm just out roamin' like I always do——" he began.

"No, you won't!" And Billy knew, from the tone of her voice, that he'd better mind her.

" 'Tain't huntin' season in the spring, nohow," said the old woman scornfully. "What kind of a boy be ye, not to know that?"

Billy knew that plenty of people hunted out of season in the mountains. Granny was still talking queer. Was she trying to mislead him?

"Well," said the boy lamely, "they most generally never ketch the fox, nohow. But I did hear hounds a-squealin'. . . ."

"Way over on Three Top likely," said Granny.

"But Pap's down here, he ain't over on Three Top. . . ." It didn't make sense. People often said Granny was queer. He began to believe it.

She made no answer, but lifted her mattock and started digging again. Sarey Sue pulled roots from the ground and shook off the dirt. Billy was afraid to move a step. He thought of Uncle Pozy and wished he'd gone the long way around by the road, so he could have avoided the Trivetts. He began to fidget. Why should they keep him standing here all day?

After a while, Sarey Sue spoke: "There's a heap o' sassy-frack down in No Man's Cove. We was aimin' to go there this fore day when we started out. We ain't a fur piece from there right now. The man's gone. Hit's safe for us to move on now, ain't hit, Gran?"

The old woman nodded. She took her almost empty snuff-box from her pocket, dipped the brush and put it in her mouth. "I reckon we might could," she said slowly. "You comin' with us?"

Billy nodded. He started out behind them. He'd go part way and turn off to Honeysuckle Hollow.

"We went this way last week, mind, Gran?" said Sarey Sue. "When that cow-brute o' ourn losted herself and we had to go out huntin' for her? Old Brindle's always gallivantin' off somewheres."

The trail was a faint one, down over rocks and boulders, below the high cliffs of the Drop-Off and through thick clumps of rhododendron and laurel. The mountains on both sides seemed to squeeze close together, their slopes getting steeper, until the valley below became a narrow ravine with a stream at the bottom.

"Let me go first," said Granny Trivett.

The boy and girl waited while she moved past them. They

came to a lively waterfall and stepped on stones to cross it. Out of hearing of the rushing water, Granny suddenly stopped. The others came up.

"Turn round and go back up the ridge," she said. "I hear men's voices."

"Hit's the timber men," said Billy. "Pap said they was workin' on this side the ridge, on Fate Merrill's place, fixin' to slide logs down a ravine near Bearskin Creek after the next freshet."

" 'Tain't timber men," said Granny firmly. "There ain't no log-roads hereabouts. Nobody's loggin' or sawmillin' round here."

"But that was Pap we seen, and he said he was loggin' over to Bearskin Creek!" protested Billy.

"Hush your loud mouth," said Granny. "Even a whisper can be heard clear acrost this holler. Come with me now." She led the boy and girl out onto a protruding rock, from where they had a clear view over the deep, shut-in valley and a wide expanse of far-off ranges lost in blue haze. "See that cliff there, with all them thicketty bushes in under it?" She pointed a bony finger.

They looked where she pointed.

"Look close now," said Granny. "See that little breath o' smoke waverin' out and around that cliff, like a thread o' steam oozin' out of a teakettle?"

The boy and girl stared.

[ 60 ]

"Now listen," she added. "Hear them voices? Men talkin'."

"I hear 'em," said Sarey Sue.

Billy nodded. "What you reckon they're up to?"

"Hit *might be* a still!" said Granny grimly. "I ain't sayin' hit is, and I ain't sayin' hit ain't, but hit *might be*."

Both Sarey Sue and Billy understood the word "still." They knew that "moonshine" was mountain whisky made in secret, because it was against the law to make it. A "still" was the place where the liquor was distilled from corn juice.

"But I thought they only made 'moonshine' by the light o' the moon," whispered Sarey Sue.

"Sometimes you're dumb, and again just plain silly," said Billy.

"Hit's less'n a mile to the Tennessee line, here," said Granny thoughtfully. "Right good location for a still."

"Why?" asked Billy.

"So when the high-sheriff comes unexpected-like, the owner can take a little step over the line and the high-sheriff can't follow him," explained Granny.

"But if a man grows more corn than he needs, and ain't got no way to sell it, what's wrong about makin' whisky out of it, if he can sell the whisky?" demanded Billy.

"Did your Pap say that?"

"Well—no, not exactly."

"That's a question each man's got to answer for hisself," said Granny, "whether he wants to go again the Law or not.

[ 61 ]

Seven years in jail is a long time to be penned up. And whisky ruins the lives of them that drinks hit."

"Let's go down and see who's runnin' the still," said Sarey Sue excitedly.

"Silly again!" sniffed Billy.

"Mercy God, gal young un!" exclaimed Granny, terrified. "You don't know what you're a-sayin'. You'd be takin' your life in your hands. Them men's got guns to point at anybody comes prowlin' round. Why, a man sits with a rifle-gun on his knee on every path leadin' to the still. 'What might be your business hereabouts, young un?' he'd say. Then he'd shoot in the air and you'd hear the grapevine of shots goin' off all the way back to the still. No, we don't go nigh it. We don't want to know who's runnin' hit."

The old woman started back up the trail. "Come *on!*" she called sharply to the two at her heels. "We don't know nothin'. We ain't seen no smoke. We ain't seen no still. We ain't seen no men—nothin'! Mind, now, *nothin'!*"

Billy remembered the figure of the man with the gun over his shoulder.

"Well, hit ain't Pap nohow. Pap ain't gone huntin' today, neither. Pap's loggin' on Bearskin Creek," he said stoutly. He started off to the right on a path through the forest.

"Don't you go runnin' off there!" called Granny. "Come back up over the ridge and go home."

"But I'm goin' to Uncle Pozy's in Honeysuckle Holler!"

protested Billy. "I been aimin' to go there all along."

"Well, you ain't!" said Granny fiercely. She seized the boy by the shoulder, pushed him ahead of her and gave him a kick.

There was nothing to do but obey.

"Git along home with ye, now, ye little ole fool!"

## CHAPTER V

## *A Split-oak Basket*

IT WAS harder and harder to get to Uncle Pozy's. The spring work began, and Pappy put more responsibility on Billy because he had to be away so much.

The timber men had slid as many logs as possible down to the foot of the mountain after the spring freshets. Now they were hauling them in wagons to market, to Mountain City in Tennessee. The road over Stone Mountain was bad and the trip often took four or five days. Pappy did not like to be away so long, for he was anxious to get the spring crops started.

"We'll plant the corn in new ground this year," he said one evening as he rose from the supper table.

"Where, Rudy?" asked Mammy.

"We'll clear off that piece right up yonder," said Pappy,

pointing out the back door to the steep mountainside above the house. "Come, son. I'll lay out your work for the next few days while I'm off haulin' them logs."

"That mountain's mighty steep for plowin'," said Mammy.

"Little Old Bet would fall shore and break her neck," said Letty Jo.

"Better plant taters up there," suggested Billy. "Ollie Holbrook says when you dig 'em, you just put your basket at the bottom, open up the row and let 'em roll down!"

"I ain't asked you-uns for your advice," said Pappy, without a smile.

Pappy was a tall, lanky man, with a brown, leathery skin and a thin, hatchet face with a strong jutting jaw. He wore brown jeans-cloth shirt and trousers, held up by cowhide suspenders. His hair showed a faint tinge of red and his eyes, of cold blue, were sharp.

"Come along, son."

They climbed up the hill.

"Your Mammy's right, Billy, hit's too steep here for plowin'," Pappy said. "So you'll have to grub hit with the maddick. Grub out all the sprouts and brambleberry vines and throw 'em in heaps for burning. Save out the sassyfrack—hit ain't good to burn the wood, and your Mammy wants the roots for tea. Letty Jo can take care of 'em. When you get the piece all cleared of sprouts, we'll burn the brush and run the harrow over it. Then we'll be ready to plant."

"But the rain will wash all the seed-corn down hill," ventured Billy.

"No, hit won't," said Pappy. "Just do as I bid you. Start off first thing tomorrow."

"Pap," said Billy, "I bet the fish air bitin' good today."

"Well, you keep right in the middle o' that row, and they won't bite *you!*" answered Pappy sternly.

Billy looked around. "How far do I dig? There ain't no fence to go by."

His father began to step off the boundaries. "After we get the corn planted, we'll get rails and lay us up a fence."

"But Pappy——"

"Now, son!" His father came closer and looked down at him. "You can fool around with them sorry, no-count boys while I'm gone if you're a mind to. . . ."

"What sorry, no-count boys?"

"Them Buckwheat Holler boys who fit you and give you that black eye."

"Oh, Burl, ye mean. Burl Moseley. He ain't got the sense of a dead crow, but he's tough as a laurel burl. I never see him—hardly ever," said Billy, smiling a little. "I licked him good. He's afeard o' me."

But Pappy was serious.

"I tell you right now, young man, you ain't gonna be a little ole sorry boy, and squirrel hunt and fish all day long. Now, young feller, I dare you to try it."

"I won't go huntin' till fall, Pap," said Billy meekly.

"Fishin' then. You mind what I say," continued Pappy. "Get this work done or take your medicine. I ain't gonna raise me up no little ole timidy men around here. Make up your mind you're gonna be tough!"

"I ain't never to fight back?" asked Billy.

"You're to fight back when they pick on you first, or insult you. But if you stay away from them Buckwheat Holler boys, they can't pick on you first," said Pappy. "Do what I say or you'll get into trouble."

The grubbing was not easy, but no harder, Billy reflected, than digging roots and herbs in the woods like the Trivetts. The boy worked steadily, but it was slow. Mammy came and helped him, while Letty Jo grubbed out the sassafras, then carried it down to the house, to scrape or "ross" the roots and dry them.

Billy worked steadily for three long days. Sometimes he

sang or whistled the ground hog song:

> "Whet up your knife and whistle up your dog,
> Whet up your knife and whistle up your dog,
> We're going to the holler to catch a ground hog,
> Ground hog! . . ."

Other songs kept popping into his head. The sun shone bright and warm, and there was no rain. The patch, as paced off by his father, was practically cleared—all but a narrow strip at one side.

"I declare!" said Mammy, when the boy came in on the third evening, his hands covered with blisters and his nose peeling with sunburn. "I declare if Billy Honeycutt ain't the workin'est boy in Hoot Owl Holler! What on earth's got into him?"

"Can I go see Uncle Pozy tomorrow?" asked Billy. It seemed a good moment to put the question.

Mammy laughed. "So that's hit! I reckon you've earned it, son. Ollie Holbrook's takin' his family over to Honeysuckle Holler to spend the day with his wife's folks. You can ride along in their jolt-wagon."

Billy threw his hat in the air and yelled for joy. He was doubly glad. He would enjoy the ride, and he wouldn't have to climb over the mountain this time. He wanted to stay as far away from No Man's Cove as possible. Granny Trivett had given him a big scare that day.

"She's only a fraidy-cat of an old woman," he said to himself, "but I druther go round by the road."

[ 68 ]

Ollie Holbrook's family were happy and jolly, and Billy liked riding with them. Ollie and his wife sat on the front seat, and their nine children, with Billy, sat some on chairs and some on the floor in the back. The jolt-wagon, pulled by two strong mules, made good time over the bumpy roads. They went through Solitude, past Jeb Dotson's store, the church-house, the post office and Hamby's mill, without stopping. Then they took the Honeysuckle Hollow road past the school-house, and after five more miles came to Uncle Pozy's, where Billy jumped down. The Holbrooks promised to stop for him on their way home in the evening, and waved him a cheery goodbye.

Billy ran right up the steep slope without stopping. "Hello! Hello, Uncle Pozy!"

There was no answer.

"Heigh-ho! Uncle Pozy! Uncle Pozy!"

Maybe he was not at home. The little one-room cabin looked deserted, except for a well-fed cat that wandered out the open door. Baskets were scattered about the room, and by the fireplace there was a great pile of splits, looped and tied in bundles. The floor was strewn with chips and looked as if it had not been swept for a month.

Billy stood on the porch and listened. Then he heard the sound of chopping. He hurried round the house and up into the woods. Not far off, he could see Uncle Pozy chopping a tree with his axe. Just as he came up, the tree leaned slowly over, and with a crash, fell to the ground.

[ 69 ]

Uncle Pozy looked at Billy and smiled. "Hit's got to be a tree of good straight grain," he said.

"Is this oak goin' to be *my* basket?" asked Billy.

"No," said Uncle Pozy. "We'll leave this un lay a while. I been workin' on another tree down to the house—peelin' off long strips of the white tough inner bark—splittin' it into 'splits' you might say. Hit's kinder tricky till you know how, but you're never too young to learn."

"Same kind o' splits you bottom chairs with?" asked Billy.

"Precisely," said Uncle Pozy. " 'Bout twelve feet long, and thin like ribbons—that's what we weave baskets with. They're all wet and slimy from the sap at first, so I hang 'em over a limb to dry. See?" He pointed to a tree near the house. "Then I fold 'em up like strips of rawhide and tie 'em in bundles, so they're easy to carry. We'll get us a bundle and I'll start you to weavin'."

"You like to do it, Uncle Pozy?"

"Law, yes," said the old man. "I been a top-notch basket-maker all my life and I know my trade. Ary kind o' basket you want I can make—large farmer's baskets for measurin' grain, small baskets for balancin' on a woman's hip or across the neck of a horse in front of the rider, pie and picnic baskets, egg baskets, mendin' and sewin' baskets, clover seed baskets, meal baskets. . . ."

"Whew!" said Billy. "Never knew there was so many kinds. Mammy says the trouble with your baskets is they never wear out."

"Shore," said Uncle Pozy. "That's why I'm so poor. Folks buy 'em once but not twice. I'm the best basket-maker on the mountain—I can make a basket so fine and close-wove, hit will hold water."

"Golly!" said Billy. "I thought only cedar buckets did that."

They came back to the house, where Uncle Pozy picked up a bundle of splits, and settled themselves to work. The old man cut a set of spokes, took up the split for a weaver and handed it to the boy.

"You can make a small one first," he said. "Keep the spokes straight and even, son, as you weave in and out. I'll help you to shape it, and finish it at the top with a fresh-cut hickory hoop that'll bend the way we want it." He went ahead with a basket of his own, keeping his eye on the boy.

It was hard work to handle the long weaver, and to keep the spokes straight, but Billy's hands were tough and he kept at it.

"Uncle Pozy," he said suddenly, "do you reckon there's any stills over Bearskin Creek way?" He must talk to somebody about the things that made Granny Trivett act so queerly.

Uncle Pozy frowned. "Might could be," he said slowly. "Plenty thicketty bushes to hide in. The laurel's so thick over yonder you can hardly see daylight at noontime. Probably full of bears too."

But Billy refused to be side-tracked. He did not want to talk about bears.

"If you knew of a still over there, what'd you do?"

Alarm filled Uncle Pozy's eyes and sharpened the tone of his voice: "Lord love ye, son, I'd stay as fur away from there as possible, and I'd say nary a word to anybody about it."

Billy pushed the weaver under the next spoke. "I wasn't hankerin' to talk to nobody but you about hit . . ." He paused, then went on quickly: "Would a good man be runnin' a still, Uncle Pozy?"

"That's hard to say, son," said the old man. "People didn't used to think it was wrong, but now hit's against the law to make corn whisky. Time was, when my Pap was young, a man could do as he pleased with the extry corn he raised, but not now no more." His voice had a sad ring to it. "Keep out o' that ere Cove, son. Hear?"

"Shore will," said Billy. He bent over his work again.

When dinnertime came, he was glad to stop. Uncle Pozy

could cook as well as make baskets. The meal of fried ham-meat and gravy, stewed apples, "leather britches" beans and corn-bread was as good as if Mammy had cooked it. After the dishes were washed up, Billy wanted to go back to his basket, but Uncle Pozy said no.

"First you must rest awhile, son. You can set and listen while I play a tune or two on my dulci-more."

"Your dulci-more?" Billy's eyes opened wide. "You'll play hit for me to hear, Uncle Pozy?"

They both used the usual mountain pronunciation of the word "dulcimer."

"Shore, son."

"Where'd you get hit? Is hit a store-bought dulci-more?"

"No, son. I made hit my own self. I like to pleasure myself with a little tune now and then."

Uncle Pozy went to the fireboard and took down the curious instrument. It looked like a long, narrow violin, with four heart-shaped sound-holes in the body. It had a long, narrow strip of wood on top, over which were strung three metal strings, with cross wires for frets.

"Oh, Uncle Pozy," cried Billy, "do you play hit like a banjo?"

"No," said the old man, sitting down. "Hit's got three strings, do, sol, do. You hold it on your knees, so, and you touch a goose quill between the wires, so, to give the tone you want. And you use this noter to play the tune." The noter was a wedge-shaped piece of wood.

"You made hit your own self?" cried Billy. "Hit ain't been bought at the store?"

"No, son," said Uncle Pozy, "I made hit outen poplar wood."

"Hit makes music like a store-bought banjo?"

"Oh, no, son," said Uncle Pozy. "Not loud and noisy like that. Hit's just a quiet little tune-box, just for soft, lonesome little tunes you play at home by yourself. Hit don't play loud dance music, like a fiddle or a banjo. You just pick it along while you're singin', like this:

> "There was an old man he had a wife,
> Dan doo, dan doo,
> There was an old man he had a wife,
> Cling-a-ma cling-a-ma clear-o;
> There was an old man he had a wife,
> And she plagued him out of his life,
> To my kum lam, slam, dam, cleary-o, Jimmy go. . . ."

"That was plumb purty," said Billy, his eyes shining.

"Now son, you try hit," said Uncle Pozy. He put the instrument on the boy's knees and explained to him just what he should do.

"Take an easy tune first. You know *Go Tell Aunt Patsy,* don't you?"

"Law, yes," said Billy, breathless.

It took some moments of trial before the strings gave forth the semblance of a tune. But at last they did, and Billy sang all six verses of *Go Tell Aunt Patsy.*

"You've got the knack, son," said Uncle Pozy happily. "Now how about workin' some more on that basket?" Abruptly, he took the dulcimer and hung it up over the fireboard. "Can't live on music all day."

Billy went back to his basket with a will, and since it was a small one, he was able to finish it with Uncle Pozy's help.

"You can make a big un next time you come," said Uncle Pozy. "A half-bushel measurin' basket—that's the easiest kind to sell."

"Hello! Hello!" came loud shouts from the road at the foot of the slope.

"That's the Holbrooks, come to take you back," said Uncle Pozy. "Skedaddle quick!"

Billy waved goodbye to the old man high up on his porch, and took his seat in the jolt-wagon. He looked down at the basket in his hand and saw not a basket, but a banjo.

His dream was more real than ever.

CHAPTER VI

## The Cowcumber Tree

BILLY was eager to go back to Uncle Pozy's again. The dogwood was in bloom all over the mountains, but cornplanting time had come, so there was no getting away.

"Uncle Pozy's plantin' his corn too," said Mammy. "In corn-plantin' time, you don't bother nobody. Corn's our livin' and everything else has to go by when hit's time to plant. If folkses don't make a crop o' corn, they go hungry."

Mammy and the children were up in the new corn patch on the side of the mountain. Mammy had brought out gourd and pumpkin seeds. "We'll plant the punkins in with the corn," she said. "They'll make good cow-feed come winter."

"Let me plant the gourds, Mammy," begged Letty Jo. "A whole row along the edge of the corn-patch."

"Law, no, gal," said Mammy. "Not there. Go sprinkle 'em in the corners of the rail fence down yonder. They have to have somethin' to climb on. Besides, they're wildy things. They don't like bein' put in a row with garden truck. Fling 'em in the briar patch in the fence corners. Then they'll make a good crop o' gourds."

Billy made furrows for the corn with his hoe. After Letty Jo had planted the gourd seed, she came to drop corn. With a bucket on her left arm, she picked out corn with her right hand and dropped it into the furrow. "I'm the fastest corn-dropper on the mountain," she bragged. "I can keep up with ary horse a-plowin' . . ."

"I ain't no horse," growled Billy, "nor mule neither."

Mammy followed with a hoe and covered the grains with dirt. Billy had to work fast to keep ahead of them.

"Fetch that basket o' seed-corn yonder, Red Top," called Letty Jo.

Red Top was a strong and active little boy. He ran, stumbled over the basket and sent it rolling and bouncing like a rubber ball, down, down the mountainside. He clapped his hands to see it.

"Lordy mercy!" cried Letty Jo, frightened. "What'll Pap say?"

"Oh, the seed-corn!" wailed Mammy. "And that's the lastest we got, too. We'll have to goose-pick hit up."

"Git them chickens off!" screamed Letty Jo. "They'll eat hit all!"

[ 77 ]

"Shoo, shoo!" Red Top and Mazie ran to chase the chickens.

Then Mazie tripped and went tumbling down hill. Letty Jo picked her up and kissed the hurt places. They all squatted down to recover the spilled seed-corn.

And just then Pappy came.

He came riding down the trail from the mountain above. When they were least expecting anyone, there beside the patch stood a horse with a rider. It was Pappy on Old Dandy.

"You give me a start, Rudolphus Honeycutt!" exclaimed Mammy, stumbling to her feet. Her face turned pale inside the deep tunnel of her sunbonnet. "Just like a ha'nt, you come so sudden."

"I'm flesh and blood, right enough," said Pappy looking down at his family. "Come just in time to see what you been a-doin' with the seed-corn."

"Hit was an accident." Billy spoke up.

"Red Top fell over the basket," put in Letty Jo.

"I didn't see it . . ." Red Top hid his face in his mother's apron and began to bawl lustily.

"Shore, the boy was just prankin'," said Pappy with a sarcastic smile. "If I had time to light down, I'd wear out a hickory on the teeny chap."

"The little rascal's not worth a pinch o' salt," said Mammy. "I'll touch a switch to him soon as we git this corn picked up." She sounded as cranky as Pap, but she pressed Red Top close and patted him on the shoulder.

"Watch out for that ole Dominicker rooster!" she screamed.

"Bless goodness, what's the matter with him? He's bloody as a hog. He's been fightin' that Wyandotte again. Why them roosters can't leave each other alone and stop fightin' when they got all the woods to range over . . ."

"They like seed-corn better, Ruthie." Pappy smiled his sarcastic smile again.

Red Top chased the rooster away, came back and squatted dutifully to pick up corn, now and then lifting a wary eye in his father's direction.

"I'm gettin' the high-sheriff after them Trivetts, Ruthie," said Pappy in a low voice. "They're all the time trespassin' on my bound o' land." Forgetting caution, he spoke louder: "Why, they think they own the whole mountain—them two. When all they got is a passel about two inches square up there, round that hut o' theirn."

"But Rudy, Gran's an old woman," said Mammy. "She's nigh ninety, if she's a day. *Nobody knows* how old she is. She might could be a hundred even."

"She ain't too old to be traipsin' all over the mountain, grubbin' up all the young trees. Anybody that takes as much as one berry offen my place, has gotta give me half of it."

"Looky here, Rudy," warned Mammy. "She might set a spell on you. There's some that says———"

"I ain't afeard of her 'witchin' me," said Pappy.

"You might say she's kin to us, too," Ruthie went on. "My uncle Vertie married that niece of Granny Trivett's, her that was Sue May Littleton."

[ 80 ]

"And you call that *kin?*"

"Hit ain't what you call *nigh* kin, but hit's *kin,* especially when all Granny's fifteen children has either died or moved to fur-off parts and forgot her, and she's only got one little chick of a grandchild left to bide with her." Ruthie's voice grew more confident. "My own Granny's dead, and so's your'n. We'd ought to look after Granny Trivett like she was *our own kin.*"

"Nonsense!" said Pappy. "Her and that gal Sarey Sue air the troublesomest pair in the mountains. I aim to put a stop to their roamin'. I'll have the high-sheriff get out a warrant for 'em, for trespassin' on my land without leave. They ain't never asked if they might could grub roots on my land. I don't like hit, and I've ordered 'em to stop time and again. Now I'll law 'em."

"They ain't got no other way to git a livin', Rudy." Mammy's voice had lost its ring of assurance. "They're poor—dirt poor."

"Why don't they bide to home and make their crops then, like other folks?" asked Pappy. "No—they go out roamin' on other folkses' land. . . ."

"*You* don't own the whole of the mountain, do you, Rudy?"

"I'm goin' down to the courthouse and git a lawyer to see how the deed reads and learn just where the boundary lays," said Pappy. "That's where I'm headin' right now. Reckon I won't be back afore night." He paused, then went on: "That old witch had the gall to say she owned that whole stretch up yonder, under that great cowcumber tree. You shoulda heard her stand there and argify about hit. Said as how she had a paper hid somewhere that she couldn't read, but she knowed hit said her Great-Granpappy owned the whole of this mountain. . . ."

"Likely he did, Rudy," said Mammy, with spirit. "He was the first settler in these here parts. Everybody knows old Great-Granpappy Goforth come over from the old country way back afore the George Washington war, 'cause he couldn't stand them kings a-rulin' over him, and raised up a big family of four wives and twenty-two young uns and was a law unto hisself. Why, everybody in these hollers and coves is some kin to him, way back somewheres."

"He takened it, you mean—just helped hisself to this mountain. But he lost hit all, bein' so shiftless and lazy, long afore Granny Trivett was ever borned," said Pappy. "More'n likely she don't own ary foot o' land at all. The deed'll prove hit. I'll get the high-sheriff to turn her out and get shet of her."

"Throw her out of the house where she's lived for nigh a hundred years? You won't do that, Rudy," said Mammy.

"She's got plenty o' kin down the country—let her go live with them." Pappy's voice was cold and harsh.

"Oh no, Rudy, she couldn't live nowheres else."

But Pappy did not seem to hear what Mammy was saying. "She's got the gall to say she owns that great cowcumber tree," he went on angrily. "I'll haul her up in court."

"What do hit matter who owns that big ole tree?" said Mammy. "Hit's been a-standin' there since long afore Great-

[ 82 ]

Granpappy Goforth ever come to these mountains. Hit'll be a-standin' there long after all us Honeycutts is under the sod."

"No, hit *won't!*" said Pappy, with a heavy frown.

"What you mean, Rudy?" cried Mammy in a frightened voice. "You ain't fixin' to chop hit . . . and log it down the mountain . . . ?" She paused, then burst out: "Granny'll law *you* if you cut down a 'boundary tree.' . . ."

Rudolphus Honeycutt suddenly noticed that his children were lined up in a row behind his wife. They were all standing solemnly, from Letty Jo down to little Mazie, big-eyed and silent, drinking in every word. Astonished and angered, he began to shout:

"Git to work, you-all! Bestir your lazy bones. See that you git all that corn planted by nightfall."

"But we ain't got enough seed-corn, Rudy," Mammy reminded him.

"You woulda had, if you hadn't spilled hit. I'll stop at the mill and fetch some," said Pappy, and then he rode down the hill and away. The *clop-clop* of Old Dandy's hoofs came echoing back behind him.

They all fell to and not a word was said until the seed-corn was picked up.

"Mammy," said Billy timidly, "you won't let Pap cut down Granny Trivett's big cowcumber tree, will you?"

"Hush your mouth, son. You'd ought to been workin' instead of listenin'." Mammy took up her hoe.

"If Pap's gone to get the high-sheriff——" the boy began again.

"Don't you worry, he won't."

"But he said he would."

"He won't," said Mammy. "He don't want to see no high-sheriff round here no more than Granny Trivett does. He's got *reasons.*"

Billy pondered. It was all very puzzling. Why did Pappy go after the high-sheriff if he didn't want him to come? Then he remembered No Man's Cove down on the far side of the ridge, directly below the cowcumber tree. Was Pappy afraid the high-sheriff might find out that something funny was going on there? Did Pap know about it, or didn't he? It was all very strange.

Billy puzzled it over and came to one conclusion. He must

warn Granny. He wasn't entirely sure of his mother. He knew her sympathies were with Granny, but she might not let him go to warn the old woman. She might be obliged to remain loyal to Pappy. Maybe that was why she said that Pap would never bring the high-sheriff. She said: Pap's got reasons. What did she mean?

When they got all the seed-corn planted, Billy asked Mammy if he could go fishing. She looked at him hard for a minute, and then said yes. She watched him from the window as he started off with his fish-line. So he had to go down to the creek and follow it upstream, as far as she could see. Then, before he got to Ollie Holbrook's place, he hid his pole and line behind a tree and struck off up through the woods. It was a rough climb because there was no trail. But, before he reached the Half-Way-Up House, he met Granny herself.

She was pulling a load of firewood on the sled.

"Where's Old Brindle?" he asked. "Can't you hitch her up and let her do that?"

"That ole cow-brute's sick," said Granny. "Sarey Sue left the shed door open and Old Brindle got in the feed-room and et a lot of cow-chop and foundered herself. Sarey Sue's gone to the store for Epsom salts. The gal's that careless, if she wasn't so big, I'd take a stick to her."

"I'll pull the sled," said the boy.

When they reached the cabin, Granny sat down on the porch step and fanned herself with her black sunbonnet. She took her box of snuff from her pocket, dipped her snuff-brush in the powder, and thrust it into her mouth. She smiled with pleasure.

Billy threw off the wood and stood up solemnly before her.

"Granny," he said, "did you know the high-sheriff's fixin' to come and set you out in the road?"

"What do you mean, boy?" asked Granny, startled.

"You better be on the lookout for the high-sheriff," said Billy. "He's a-comin' with a warrant to haul you to court for trespassin' on my Pap's land. Pap wants to get shet of you and Sarey Sue. I heard him tell Mammy about hit, and I run off to warn you."

"Oh, that!" Granny leaned back and cackled with laughter. "You mean that argyment with your Pap about the old cow-cumber tree. Don't you worry none, son. I'm a good match for your Pap. He won't bring no high-sheriff round here—not till the creeks start runnin' uphill! Why, I recollect when your Pap was a little tyke and wore diapers. His Mam said he was the most headstrong of all her children. He'd find a big rock and go buttin' his head agin it. . . ."

"But he rode off to the county seat this fore day," said Billy.

"Mark my words, son, I ain't skeered a mite. There ain't no high-sheriff a-comin' round this mountain. I needn't worry and neither does your Pap." Granny laughed again.

Billy felt relieved of his fears. Granny, he knew, was a wise old woman. Mammy had said the same thing, so the two of them must be right. It was with a lighter heart that he went singing down the mountain and came home again.

Mammy must have known where he went, because she forgot to ask him if he'd caught any fish. He put his pole and line on the back porch and said nothing.

It was night-time, as Pappy had said it would be, when he returned from the county seat. He brought the seed-corn with him.

The first question Mammy put to him was: "When is the high-sheriff a-comin'?"

"He ain't a-comin'," said Pappy. "He 'lowed that there was easier ways to handle Granny Trivett. We searched and found the deed and the lawyer down there made me a copy of it. Hit says my east line goes 'up the side of Laurel Mountain to the top of the ridge, then westward to a poplar, then to an old fence row at an agreed corner, then down the hill to a stake in John Holbrook's line'—John was Ollie's grandfather. 'Westward to a poplar' hit says. That's the tree."

"But the cowcumber tree ain't a poplar," said Mammy. "Likely hit means a tulip tree. Lumbermen are always callin' a tulip tree a yellow poplar."

Pappy did not listen. "I'll read the deed to Granny Trivett and prove to her that tree belongs to me, and my line goes past hit to an old fence corner and down the mountainside from there, and she'd better not trespass this side of hit."

"You reckon Old Gran's such a fool she don't know the difference between a cowcumber and a tulip tree?" asked Mammy. "Why, the cowcumber's flowers is big and white like a magnolia, and the tulips' are red and yellow. . . ."

[ 88 ]

But again Pappy did not listen.

Billy felt happy again. He did not care whether it was a cowcumber or a tulip tree. The high-sheriff wasn't coming, and there were only a few more rows of seed-corn to plant. Then corn-planting would be over and he could go to Uncle Pozy's again.

CHAPTER VII

## A Knock at the Door

"Go tell Aunt Patsy,
Go tell Aunt Patsy,
Go tell Aunt Patsy
The old gray goose is dead.

The one that she's been saving,
The one that she's been saving,
The one that she's been saving
To make a feather bed.

She died in the mill-pond,
She died in the mill-pond,
She died in the mill-pond
Standing on her head . . ."

BUT OUR old goose *hain't* dead," cried Sarey Sue, running out, "and we are a-goin' to sleep in feathers *some* day!"

Billy had climbed the trail quietly, and now he sat on the top step of Granny Trivett's porch, with his dulcimer across his knees. He twanged on the instrument and sang lustily. Granny came running out too.

"Billy!" they cried. "A dulci-more! Whose is it?"

"Mine," said Billy proudly. "I made hit myself. Uncle Pozy helped. When I got two big measurin' baskets made, Uncle Pozy said I might could have a little fun. So we made my dulci-more and he learned me a tune or two to play on hit."

"Sing, Billy, sing!" cried Sarey Sue, clapping her hands. "Let's have us some purty music."

"Come in and have a chair, son," said Granny. They went in and listened while Billy finished his song:

> "The goslings all are crying,
> The goslings all are crying,
> The goslings all are crying
> To think their mother's dead.
>
> The gander is a-mourning,
> The gander is a-mourning,
> The gander is a-mourning
> Because his wife is dead.
>
> The barnyard is a-weeping,
> The barnyard is a-weeping,
> The barnyard is a-weeping
> Waiting to be fed."

Billy looked up, but Granny and Sarey Sue did not clap their hands. "I wisht it had been that ole goose o' Saphronia Lyle's that died," said Granny.

"So we couldn't never sleep in feathers?" Sarey Sue looked about ready to cry.

Billy wondered what was the matter, but they did not explain. They went right on with their work. The floor was covered with roots and bark. Sarey Sue was "rossing" roots—scraping the outer skin off—while Granny was sorting dried herbs and putting them into meal sacks. Outside, the porch floor was covered with herbs spread out to dry on cloths in the sun.

But Sarey Sue could not stay sad for long.

"We're aimin' to go tradin' at Jeb Dotson's store soon," she said after a while. "Our house is so messed up with yarbs, there ain't no place to walk or eat or sleep. Gotta get hit cleared out."

"What you tradin' for?" asked Billy, his eyes twinkling. "A banjo?"

"Law no, I got my Pappy's accordion," said Sarey Sue.

Granny filled her corncob pipe with dried tobacco and lighted it with a coal from the hearth. "Now you got you a dulci-more, son," she said between puffs, "I reckon you ain't cravin' no store-bought banjo no more."

"What you think I'm makin' baskets for?" asked Billy. "Little ole dulci-more ain't good for much—just for little soft ole baby tunes and barnyard ditties. Just for songs to set and listen to. Hit ain't loud enough for dance music. . . ."

[ 92 ]

"So ye're hankerin' to play for dances, Bill Honeycutt!" cackled Granny. "Soon ye'll be a-talkin' to a purty gal."

The boy hung his head. "Gotta get my banjo first," he said.

"Don't aim for the moon, son," said Granny. "A banjo costs nigh as much as a cow-brute."

"Hit do?" The boy's eyes opened wide. "Then hit'll take a heap o' baskets. Likely I'll wear my fingers to the bone." He looked at the herbs. "What you folks tradin' your yarbs for? Looks like you got enough to buy Jet Dotson out."

Sarey Sue looked at her Granny, but the old woman bent over and did not answer.

"I might could get me a new calico dress this time," Sarey Sue ventured in faint voice. Her thin, pretty face glowed pink. "With purties all over hit . . . I ain't never had none. . . ."

Granny sat up, her back as straight as a board. "Who said you was gettin' a new dress—*a store-bought dress?* What you wantin' a new dress for—to wear in the briar patch and get tore to rags?"

Sarey Sue wilted. Scraping the root in her hand vigorously, her knife slipped and made a cut on one finger. "I'll put coon-root on hit. That'll stop the bleedin'." She looked at her Granny. "I could wear my new dress to one of them square dances down at Solitude. . . ."

"Think you're growed, do ye?" The old woman took a few puffs on her pipe. "Lordy mercy! Wantin' store-bought clothes. What's the world a-comin' to?" She frowned at the girl. "Fixin' to go steppin' out frolickin', eh? Well, you'll stay home and take that piece o' brown check linsey I wove last winter and get busy with your finger-sewin'."

Sarey Sue began to sulk. "Law me, I'm plumb tired o' goin' round in rags," she complained. "Dirty ole brown linsey, the color o' dried-up yarbs."

"Hush your foolish talk, gal young un," said Granny. "Time you was learnin' to weave linsey yourself. Granpappy's loom sets idle most of the time now, gatherin' dust and cobwebs. Time was, when I was your age, ye'd hear the old treadles a-thumpin' from morn till night. Me and my Mammy and my sisters never give that loom no rest. Store-bought clothes! *Why, the world's turned right around now, to what hit used to be!*"

"What's turned hit around, Granny?" asked Billy.

Granny studied for a moment before she spoke.

"SIN!" she cried.

Billy and Sarey Sue looked startled at the suddenness of her reply.

"I know the Bible from cover to cover, even if I can't read," said the old woman. "Sarey Sue makes a stab o' readin' hit to me, but she ain't been to school long enough, all them long words they stump her. But I know for a fact, folks is more wicked than they used to be. My Pappy never drunk two spoonsful of liquor in his life, and my Mammy was a good woman. When she was took sick, she was plumb out of her mind until the last day, when she was clear as anybody. I sot up day and night for nine weeks, takin' care of her. When other folkses come in to wait on her, she'd say: 'Jule, where's Jule?' My name's Julie, but she called me Jule. Hit was the touchingest thing I ever saw, that fore day, when she said: 'I want to shake hands and tell you goodbye, Jule.' Them was her lastest words."

Granny Trivett sniffled and wiped her nose on her apron.

"New dress!" she suddenly exploded. "Gotta buy us a new cow, now Old Brindle's dead."

Sarey Sue looked ready to cry again.

"Old Brindle died?" asked Billy. Now he understood why they were so sad when he first came in.

"Hark!" Granny sat up briskly in her chair, while her herbsack dropped to the floor beside her. "I hear the hoofbeats of somebody's nag. Somebody's dyin' or havin' a baby. Look-see who's a comin'."

Sarey Sue ran to the door and looked out and down.

"Hit's a strange man, Granny, on a big white nag. I ain't never seed him afore—or his nag. He's big and fat and——"

"Come inside. Shut the door. Tight!" ordered Granny. Calmly she took the pipe out of her mouth and with a few sharp knocks, emptied the ashes on the stone hearth.

Sarey Sue stood with her mouth open and her long thin arms hanging loosely at her sides. Billy picked up his dulcimer and started for the back door.

"Stay here, son," said Granny. "Don't speak a word, but do as I bid ye."

The man had tied his horse to a tree at the edge of the

clearing, and they could hear his footsteps crossing the fore yard, then coming slowly up the steps and across the porch.

They stood still, listening. It seemed to take a long time for him to reach the door.

"He never hollered," whispered Sarey Sue.

"Hush up!" said Granny.

Then came a loud knock at the door.

The sound was ominous. The neighbors always called out and rarely knocked at a door in the mountain country. The door usually stood open, summer and winter, as a sign of welcome.

"Hit's the high-sheriff, Granny," whispered Billy. "Pap must a told him to come, nohow. Better not go to the door or he'll hand you a paper, and if you tetch it, he'll haul you

and Sarey Sue off to jail. Let's all scoot out the back door."

"Gran!" whispered Sarey Sue, shaking like a leaf, "if we run up the mountain and go in a rock-house, he can't never find us."

"Here, hide, you-uns," said Granny. She took an armful of quilts off the chest by the loom and threw them over Sarey Sue, and a pile of dried herbs over Billy.

The man knocked again, and the knock was so noisy, it echoed through the house.

"I ain't runnin' from nobody," said Granny Trivett in a loud voice, loud enough to be heard through the closed door.

She tied the knot in her head-handkerchief tightly. Slowly she removed her soiled dark apron, took a clean white one from a hook and tied it round her waist. Then she went to the door. She opened it a crack and poked her nose out.

"Who be ye?" she demanded. She may have been brave and courageous, but her voice sounded trembly. "Where ye from?"

The man took off his hat and said, "My name is Ellis and I've just come from the county seat."

"Ye ain't from the mountains," Granny went on, "or I'd a seen ye before. So ye're one of them city fellers . . ."

The man, middle-aged and heavy set, had a genial face. He smiled a little. "City or country is all the same to me," he said.

"Shucks!" said Granny. "Even if ye come from the out-land and got book-larnin' and store-bought clothes, we're just as good as ye air, if not a whole sight better."

"I haven't the least doubt of it, ma'am," said the stranger.
"I have long admired the mountain people, especially for their
spirit of independence. And today—I only wanted to ask a
question or two."

But Granny was not to be disarmed so easily. "Be ye the
Law?"

Again the man smiled a little.

"I only wanted to ask where Rudolphus Honeycutt lives,"
he said gently. "They told me at the store to come up Roundabout valley."

"Ye've come to . . ." A warning rustle of herbs stopped her.

"Never heard tell o' him," said Granny glibly.

"But he's lived in Hoot Owl Hollow all his life, on the
farm his father had before him," insisted the stranger.

"This ain't Hoot Owl Holler," said Granny.

"Where is it then?"

"Down there." She nodded her head vaguely toward the
valley below.

"I have been told there's a still somewhere on this mountain," the man went on. "You don't happen to know——"

"Then ye BE the Law!" said Granny. "I knowed hit the
minute I sot eyes on ye!"

"Have you ever seen——" began the man.

"If there's a still somewhere on this mountain," said Granny
Trivett angrily, "I don't know where 'tis, and I don't know
who runs it, and I don't want to know where 'tis nor who
runs it. And if I did know where 'tis and who runs it, I

[ 98 ]

wouldn't tell *you!*"

"Thank you, ma'am." Seeing that it was useless to question her further, the stranger put his hat back on his head and made his way off the porch.

*Ker-chew! Ker-chew!* Billy pushed the herbs aside and came up sneezing.

"Did ye sniff some sneeze-weed, son?" asked Granny.

*Ker-chew! Ker-chew! Ker-chew!*

Sarey Sue stuck her frightened face out from under the quilts and said, "I hear shootin'—let's run!"

"He's gone," said Granny, still sputtering. "I got shet of him mighty quick."

*Ker-chew! Ker-chew!* Billy sneezed again.

"Shucks! Just you sneezin'," exclaimed Sarey Sue. "I thought

hit was the man shootin'. Here, try poke-weed instead of sneeze-weed . . ."

Billy grabbed it and started after her. "I'll poke poke-weed down your throat, I'll——"

Granny came away from the door and sat down in a chair, suddenly weak. Sarey Sue stepped up beside her. "What did he come for, Gran?"

"Law, I don't know," replied Granny.

"Reckon he'll find out where Pap lives?" asked Billy. "What do you s'pose he wants to see Pap for?"

"Law, I don't know," said Granny, "and I don't want to know."

"Reckon hit's about that cowcumber tree and the deed?" persisted Billy.

"Law, I don't know and I don't want to know," said Granny.

"Reckon that was a still we saw that day, back in under that big cliff? Reckon that's the one he's huntin' for?"

"Law, I don't know," said Granny. "Stop askin' questions. I'm plumb wore out. I ain't got no more spirit than a little ole gate-post."

"Reckon he was the high-sheriff from the county seat?" Billy went on.

Granny did not answer. She looked tired. She reached for her snuff, dipped a good brushful and leaned back to rest.

"Shucks, no," said Sarey Sue. "He never set us out in the road, he never talked 'bout no cowcumber tree, he never put us in no jail for trespassin'. He didn't do nary them things your Pappy said he was fixin' to do, so he couldn't a been the Law."

Billy looked at Sarey Sue with new respect, surprised at her clear reasoning. She wasn't dumb or silly this time.

"That air a true word, Sarey Sue," he said.

"The high-sheriff wears a big shiny badge," added Granny.

"Oh!" said Billy. "Then he wasn't the high-sheriff."

"But sometimes it's hid under his coat."

"Oh!" said Billy. "Then was he or wasn't he? And if he wasn't, then who was he?"

"Lordy mercy, don't ask me!" said Granny.

It was more puzzling than ever to Billy. If the man wasn't the high-sheriff, who could he be? Granny was being stubborn. These were things she refused to talk about. He might as well go home. He picked up his dulcimer and looked at it. Only a short time ago he had been so happy, playing it and singing. Now all his happiness was gone. The sun had been swallowed up by a big black cloud. His head ached. He must go home.

Then fear came.

Maybe the stranger had found out where his father lived. Maybe he had stopped at Pap's house. What would he stop at Pap's house for?

Pap was a good man. He went logging every day. He hauled logs to Mountain City. Pap never quarreled with anybody— only with Granny Trivett about the cowcumber tree, and that was nothing. People often quarreled over boundaries when they weren't sure just where they were located. Uncle Pozy said only lawless men made corn liquor nowadays. Pap would never break the law. Mammy wouldn't let him. Mammy would . . . but what could Mammy do about it?

Granny began to sing. What did she have to sing for, at a time like this? Then, in spite of himself, Billy was listening:

"Wake up, wake up, darlin' Cory!
What makes you sleep so soun'?
The revenoo officers' a-comin'
Gonna tear your still-house down.

I'm goin' across the deep ocean,
I'm goin' across the deep sea,
I'm goin' across the deep ocean,
Just to bring darlin' Cory to me.

Gonna dig me a hole in the meadow,
Gonna dig me a hole in the groun',
Gonna dig me a hole in the meadow,
Just to lay darlin' Cory down.

Don't you hear the bluebirds a-singin'?
Don't you hear the mournful sound?
They're a-preachin' Cory's fun'ral,
In some lonesome graveyard ground . . ."

The song made him feel sadder than ever. Granny must have known how troubled he was. She began to stir about. "Let me fix you some sassyfrack tea, son," she said. "Hit'll give you strangth."

Billy felt better after he drank the tea and ate a big piece of corn-bread. But all the way, running down the trail, he felt as if a heavy load had been placed on his shoulders, so heavy he could not shake it off.

"What you runnin' from, son? Booger man chasin' you?"

Mammy was there, just inside the kitchen door, lighting the lamp.

"Pap home yet?" he asked.

"No, he ain't," said Mammy.

"Did a strange man come to the door, askin' for Pappy?"

Mammy kept on looking at the lamp, as she turned the wick lower, to keep from blacking the chimney. She gave herself plenty of time to think what to say.

"Well, did he?"

"No," said Mammy.

She said only that one word. Then she shut her lips tight.

Billy slouched off to bed. Mammy wouldn't talk either. That made it still worse.

CHAPTER VIII

## *Jeb Dotson's Store*

"You gotta walk that lonesome valley,
You gotta walk it all alone;
Ain't nobody gonna walk it for ye,
You gotta walk it by yourself . . ."

WHOA mule! Whoa, I say!"
Billy tied Old Bet to the hitching rack, took his baskets
off her back and carried them into the store.

The store looked just the same inside, even though it had
been switched roundabout. There in the far corner, back
of the counter, was Jeb Dotson's bed, unmade. A sheet-iron
stove, cold and fireless now, sat in the center, its rickety stove-
pipe running into a chimney which stood out in the room.
The rear of the store was shrouded in a curtain of leather
harness, hanging from the ceiling.

On a barrel just inside the door stood Jeb's phonograph, with its big horn shaped like a giant morning-glory. Jeb had just put a record on and wound the crank. Now the lively tune *The Bird on Nellie's Hat* blared forth noisily.

Billy stood and stared at it, listening with all ears. He could never get over the wonder of it—music coming out of a box. He was always ready to think up an excuse that would take him to the store, just so he could see and hear it.

"Hi, bud!" Joe Farley, Jim Hardin and some other men, leaning on the back counter, were watching him. "Hi, bud!" called Pappy Weaselface.

Jeb Dotson was selling millinery now. He placed a lady's hat on a painted, wooden head on the side counter. He looked up and frowned. "What you up to, Bill Honeycutt?" he asked crossly. "Tryin' to run Uncle Pozy outa business?"

"I made 'em my own self," said Billy. "Uncle Pozy showed me how."

"The little ground hog made 'em his own self!" echoed Pappy Weaselface. Pappy's real name was Watson, but he came by his nickname because his face was small and pinched like a weasel's. He was from Buckwheat Hollow and always seemed to have leisure to loaf at the store.

The men laughed. Billy wondered what was funny. The record on the phonograph finished and the music ended.

"What are you going to do with your baskets, boy?" asked a woman's voice.

Billy looked up. A strange lady stood by the counter. She

wore a dark skirt, a white shirtwaist, and a straight sailor hat. Her hair curled softly about her face and her eyes were kind.

Billy hung his head for a moment. Then he looked up and said shyly, "Trade 'em in, ma'am."

"Your Mammy out of sugar and coffee?" asked Jeb Dotson.

"Law no. I ain't tradin' for her, I'm tradin' for my own self," said Billy stoutly.

"The little rabbit's tradin' for his own self!" echoed Joe Farley.

The men laughed again.

"Well, I don't need no more baskets," broke in Jeb Dotson crossly. "I've got more baskets than I can sell in a month of Sundays. Uncle Pozy come by here t'other day, loaded down like a pack mule and wished all his'n on me. Can't take no more till I get shet of what I got."

It was true—a whole row of baskets hung from the low ceiling in front of the dangling harness. Billy's heart sank. He looked at the second-hand banjo hanging on the wall near the front window. It was so beautiful. As long as it hung there, he would not lose hope.

Then he thought of Uncle Pozy. Uncle Pozy made his living selling baskets. If Uncle Pozy didn't sell baskets, he could not eat. It was good of Uncle Pozy to teach him—but maybe it was all wrong. Maybe he was taking trade away from Uncle Pozy.

He set the baskets carefully on the floor. He had worked so hard and been so proud of them. He sat down on an overturned nail keg and rested his chin in his hand. He had to think things over.

"Your Pap come back yet?"

It was Walt Moseley who put the question. He had just come in, swinging a bunch of chickens by their legs, in each hand. The hens began to flap their wings and cackle noisily.

"Nope," said Billy.

"He's away from home right smart now, ain't he?" The man's eyes narrowed.

"Yep," said Billy.

That was another worry. Why didn't Pap stay home? He'd been away, off and on, ever since that strange man came to ask for him. Mammy refused to answer questions, and went around with her lips closed tight, as if she were holding a secret in.

Jeb wound up the phonograph and *The Bird on Nellie's Hat* began to play again. Walt Moseley joined the men at the back of the store. Together they talked in low voices, now and then looking in Billy's direction. The boy forgot them as he listened to the music.

"Lordy mercy! How's a body to git histed up?"

A cackling voice outside the door made everybody look. There were the Trivetts, Granny and Sarey Sue, loaded down with sacks of herbs on shoulders and hips. They must have walked all the way down the mountain.

Billy jumped to his feet and gave them each a hand, pulling them up into the doorway. Then he sat down and stared

[ 109 ]

at the floor again. The song on the phonograph ended abruptly.

Billy lifted his head when he heard a strain of music outside the door. Burl Moseley came strolling in, picking his father's guitar. The brown-and-white-spotted horse was hitched to the rack out in front.

Jeb Dotson greeted the Moseleys while the Trivetts waited.

"New shoes," shouted Walt Moseley, after he had dumped his hens in a pen at the back of the store. "New shoes for Burl and me."

They stuck their feet into the shoes Jeb brought out, and paraded around the floor. Sarey Sue could not keep her eyes off the shiny footwear. Walt saw Granny Trivett and went over to talk to her.

"Lizy's took bad with a misery in her stomach," he said. "Can you come over and bring somethin' to cure her?"

"She's got yarbs, ain't she?" inquired Granny. "What is it this time?" They went into a whispered consultation.

Burl twanged the strings of his guitar and came over where
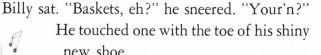
Billy sat. "Baskets, eh?" he sneered. "Your'n?" He touched one with the toe of his shiny new shoe.

"Keep your feet offen my baskets!" said Billy angrily.

Burl gave the basket a kick that sent it spinning across the floor. The next minute Billy was after him. Burl went tearing out the door and hid around the corner of the building.

"He don't want to fight this time," said Sarey Sue, grinning.

"Law, no," said Billy, dusting his hands off. "He ain't forgot that licking I gave him. He ain't got the wits of a pet coon."

"He's got a guitar," said Sarey Sue. She pronounced it git'-tar. "He's got new shoes too."

"Law, yes," said Billy, sitting down on the keg again. "I'll spoil them purty new shoes o' his'n, sure as sun-up!"

Walt Moseley went to the back of the store and the men laughed noisily. Walt was friendly to all. He slapped the men on the back.

"Shoes feel good?" asked Jeb Dotson.

"Toler'ble" laughed Walt.

The storekeeper approached the strange lady. "What for you, Miz Sutherland, ma'am?" he asked. "A purty new hat?"

Everybody in the store looked at her. A whisper of gossip went around. Walt Moseley whispered it to Granny Trivett and Sarey Sue repeated it to Billy:

"Her name's Miz Lucy Sutherland and she's from Asheville. She come on the train to Cranberry, and rid all the way over here in the mail-wagon. She's stayin' at the Wilcox's in Sugar Grove—they're kin to Jerusha Wilcox on Cabbage Creek, and they brung her over here. She's waitin' till Jerusha comes back from visitin' her sister-in-law, old Hamby's niece, who keeps house for him . . ."

Everybody waited to see what Lucy Sutherland would buy.

But she disappointed them all by buying nothing. "I'm just waiting," she said.

Then Jeb Dotson remembered his manners and brought her a chair and she sat down. Pappy Weaselface and some of the men went out and it seemed quieter after that. Billy listened to the babble of the creek through the open door.

"Bring your yarbs over here," called Jeb Dotson.

Granny Trivett and Sarey Sue walked over to the scales in the corner. They stood by uneasily, as Jeb opened each sack, looked inside, sniffed, and pinched the contents with his fingers. One sack he took to the door, and without a word, dumped it into the creek.

"O-o-o-oh!" wailed Sarey Sue.

"Hush up!" said Granny. "I told you poke-root never gets dry."

Jeb weighed the sacks one by one and looked at the scales. Then he went to the desk behind the counter and wrote some figures down.

Lucy Sutherland was looking at a roll of flowered calico. Sarey Sue slid over. "That's plumb purty, ain't hit?" she breathed.

"Are you going to buy a new dress?" the lady asked.

The girl did not answer. She hung her head, overcome with shyness. Lucy Sutherland asked the question again.

"Law, no," said Sarey Sue. Her shyness overcome, she grew talkative. "I don't never wear store-bought clothes—only linsey that Granny weaves on the loom, and cotton-check for aprons. Gran says cotton-check s cheaper and wears longer'n calico. I been cravin' a calicker dress since I was a knee-baby, I reckon, but usually we get somethin' else. One time Granny had to have a new fryin' pan, 'cause the handle on the old un got broke. Another time we got a hip basket to tote yarbs down off the mountain. Last year, Gran had to have new shoes, 'cause her poor old feetses is so tender. Seems like we're always cravin' somethin'. If hit ain't one thing, hit's two."

"You don't wear shoes?" asked the lady, looking down at the girl's bare feet.

"Law, no," said Sarey Sue. "My feetses is tough. I can go right up the mountain and walk in a briar patch. Course I always look where I'm a-goin' and don't step in no bull-nettles. 'Twas a bull-nettle killed my Uncle Fred, Pappy's brother. He was cuttin' wood on the Peak a long time ago and

[ 113 ]

touched one, and them little ole nettles stung his hand, and he took blood pizen and hit killed him."

"Better not step on no rattlesnakes, Sarey Sue," warned Billy.

"Shore won't," said the girl, laughing. She turned to the lady. "That's Billy Honeycutt," she explained, pointing her thumb at the boy. "He's cravin' that banjo——"

"Shut up, gal, don't you go tellin' that," growled Billy.

"Come, Sarey Sue." Granny bustled up. "Let's go. H'ist that poke up and we'll light out for home." She placed a sack of wheat flour on the girl's shoulder.

"But ain't I . . ." Sarey Sue's skinny hand still touched the piece of calico. "I might could——"

"Get along, Sarey Sue." Granny Trivett's face fairly shone with happiness. She patted the two patch-pockets on her cotton-check apron. Both were bumpy-looking, pinned tightly shut with two safety-pins above the bumps.

Sarey Sue dropped the calico and stared. "Did you get a heap o' cash money?"

"I takened a poke o' white flour and a box of snuff," said Gran, "and he give me the rest all in silver. That makes hit seem twicet as much. With what's hid at home, we'll soon have enough to buy us a new cow-brute. . . ."

Sarey Sue said nothing. As she lifted the heavy sack to her other shoulder, her eyes filled with tears.

"Ain't you proud we got us a poke o' white flour, Sarey Sue?" asked Granny.

[ 114 ]

Still the girl did not speak.

"Just think of all the biscuit-bread we'll be eatin', gal."

No reply.

"We been hungry for biscuit-bread the whole endurin' winter, Sarey Sue," Granny went on. "You hustle on home now and make us some."

"Don't want none," mumbled Sarey Sue.

"You're a master-hand for notions, gal," scolded Granny, as they jumped from the high doorstep.

Billy had heard it all. He knew just how Sarey Sue felt. She had set her heart on a calico dress, just as he had set his on a banjo. But nice things like that never happened. Maybe Granny was right. Maybe store-bought clothes were wicked. Granny never bought anything except what she had to have to keep the two of them alive. Calico dresses and banjos were extra things. They were not things you had to have to keep alive, but things that made you *want* to be alive.

Billy looked out the window. Granny climbed on the back of the Moseley horse and rode away, while Sarey Sue, with the sack of flour on her shoulder, stood and watched her go.

Then Billy heard Jeb Dotson speaking: "Let's see your baskets, young feller."

The boy picked up the basket which Burl Moseley had kicked across the floor. He set them all in a row on the counter.

"What's your Mammy want for 'em—sugar, salt, flour?" asked Jeb.

"I'm tradin', not my Mammy," said Billy firmly.

[ 115 ]

"What you want—coffee?"

"No, I don't want no household truck, I want money."

"Your Pap know about this tradin' of yours?" asked Jeb.

"Well no, I ain't told him yet. How much can I have? I'll take hit in silver like Granny Trivett, so's I can hear it rattle in my pocket."

"Think you're gettin' a fortune, eh?" laughed Jeb.

Jeb seemed friendly again, like he did the day the spring freshet turned his store roundabout. Or, was it only because Lucy Sutherland was listening? You never could tell about Jeb, whether he was your friend or not.

There was the banjo, hanging by the window, glittering like a ripe gourd in the sun.

"Oh Jeb!" cried Billy, his eyes sparkling. "I'm cravin' that banjo more'n anything else in the world. Will you trade hit for my baskets?"

"Law no!" snorted Jeb angrily. He spat on the floor behind the counter. "That banjo's worth *money.*"

"Well, give me money then."

"You little ole fool, I can't give you money," growled Jeb. "You'd have to make baskets till Judgment Day before you'd earn that banjo."

Jeb was cranky again. Billy realized he shouldn't have mentioned the banjo.

Jerusha Wilcox came in and Lucy Sutherland got up off her chair, but she wasn't ready to go yet. She asked Jerusha to wait a while longer.

"I'll tell you what I'll do," said Jeb, now conscious of his audience. "I'll give you credit."

"What's that?"

"I'll write it down in my book—the amount you get—each time I sell one of your baskets. I'll write it down and tot it up. And when you've got enough for the banjo, I'll tell you."

Billy thought it over. The offer seemed fair enough.

"But I wanted money," he said.

"You might lose silver, or have it stole," warned Jeb, "and then where'd you get a banjo? Credit's the same as money that I'm keepin' for you—keepin' safe."

"But somebody might could come in and buy the banjo with money," said Billy, "before I get enough baskets made."

"They might could." Jeb shrugged his shoulders. "But not

likely. Nobody in the mountains has got money."

Billy knew that was true. Only Granny Trivett with her pockets full to buy a new cow. And nobody could steal that because she had it fastened in safe with safety-pins.

"You'll get your credit *when the baskets sell,*" said Jeb.

Billy wished Jerusha Wilcox and Lucy Sutherland would go, but they didn't. They seemed to be waiting for him to leave first.

He walked slowly out the door, his shoulders hunched. Those last words of Jeb's kept echoing through his mind: *"When the baskets sell . . ." "When the baskets sell . . ."* He couldn't forget that long row of Uncle Pozy's baskets, hanging from the ceiling of the store, that would have to sell first.

Billy walked slowly toward the hitching rack, when suddenly, out from the corner of the building sprang Burl Moseley. "Where's my horse?" he demanded.

Billy laughed. "Don't you know your Mam's sick and your Pappy told Granny Trivett to go take care of her?"

"If that Sarey-gal's racin' my horse again, I'll, I'll——"

"Granny Trivett's takened your nag, I tell you," repeated

Billy. "How else could she get all the way over to Buckwheat Holler? Are you dumb as a dead crow?"

"Don't you dare insult me!" shouted Burl. He jumped on Billy and threw him to the ground. They rolled over in a fight.

"Got a git-tar, have you?" yelled Billy. "Let me break hit over your dumb head. Got new shoes, have you? Go soak 'em in a mud puddle."

The guitar was nowhere to be seen, but the new shoes were badly scuffed by the time the fight was over and Burl was left lying in the road. Billy dusted his hands off and walked away.

Not till he got back to the hitching rack did he notice that Old Bet was gone.

Then he saw her—Sarey Sue on the little gray mule, with the sack of flour perched up in front of her. She had gone off up the Honeysuckle Hollow road and was coming back. Miss Viney, the postmistress, appeared just as Jerusha Wilcox and Lucy Sutherland came out of the store. Mrs. Pappy Weaselface and her four children got down from a wagon that had just come over and stopped.

"Lordy mercy!" Mrs. Pappy put her hands on her hips and stared. "A gal young un a-ridin' a mule, and a-straddle at that!"

She laughed, and the other women laughed too, as Sarey Sue went trotting by.

Billy turned away. Women-folks just didn't ride mules nor

sit astride. Sarey Sue was always doing something dumb or silly, and getting herself laughed at. This was even worse than riding other people's horses. She'd been waiting around, so he would see her. Let her take Old Bet—Billy did not care.

He drew a deep breath and walked on.

> "You gotta walk that lonesome valley,
> You gotta walk it all alone;
> Ain't nobody gonna walk it for ye
> You gotta walk it by yourself . . ."

The words: *You got to walk that lonesome valley* kept repeating themselves over and over. A banjo! He'd better forget it—it was an impossible dream. And baskets. Hardest things in the world to make and no sale for them, because all the mountain people had plenty of their own. Why work so hard?

Billy looked up to see where he was. He hadn't taken the Roundabout Creek road at all. He had started off in the opposite direction to get away from Sarey Sue, and here he was, well on the road to Last Hope Hollow where Uncle Jamie lived. Uncle Jamie and the boys. He hadn't seen them for a long time.

It was wonderful at Uncle Jamie's house. They were all so glad to see him. It was just dinnertime when he got there.

"Come set your feet under the table," called Aunt Tallie in her cheerful voice.

The invitation brought them all running. Billy sat beside Glen, and Rick beside Jack on the long side benches, with

Uncle Jamie at the head. Aunt Tallie and Ettie Bell began
to pile fried chicken on their plates, fill their glasses with
buttermilk and pass biscuits, hot from the oven every minute
or two. Now and then Ettie Bell waved the paper fly-brush
over their heads, to shoo the flies away.

After dinner, Billy told them about his dulcimer, and that
got them started on their songs. They were the "singingest
family" in the county, everybody said. They sang old songs
and made up new ones of their own. Some of their songs
were sad and mournful, but many of them were funny. They
sang some funny ones today and Billy just had to laugh.

Uncle Jamie got out his fiddle and played. Even though
there were crops to make, Uncle Jamie sat down and fiddled
and patted his foot as if he hadn't a care in the world.

Billy watched, fascinated. "How do you do it, Uncle Jamie?"

"Well, you just scatter about and pick up a tune," said Uncle Jamie, smiling, "and then you rattle hit out with your fingers and the bow. You don't use notes, you just play by the feel of it. . . . If you ever want to try hit, son, I'll learn you how."

Billy liked the new song that Glen and Rick had made up, and he sang it all the way home:

> "Rye straw,
> Rye straw,
> Rye straw!
> I wish I had a thousand bricks
> To build my chimney higher,
> To keep the neighbors' cussed cats
> From scratching out my fire!
> Rye straw,
> Rye straw,
> Rye straw!
> I bored a hole in Brindle's horn,
> And there I tied a string;
> I led her to the river side
> And there I plunged her in!
> Rye straw,
> Rye straw,
> Rye straw!"

CHAPTER IX

# The Hound Pup

WHAT YOU doin', son?" asked Mammy.

"Just a-lookin' at the wish-book," answered Billy. He was stretched out on the porch, his chin cupped in his hands, with the open mail-order catalogue before him. One page showed banjos and the other guitars.

"Don't set your heart on the moon, son," said Mammy.

She sat down in the split-oak rocker and took up her mending. Billy hadn't told Mammy what he was looking at. He wondered if she knew. If he couldn't get the banjo in Jeb Dotson's store, he'd send away to the mail-order house and buy one. But first he'd have to get money for his baskets.

The sound of squeaking wagon wheels down in the valley reached his ears. His mother turned her head and listened too.

"Hit might could be Pappy a-comin' home," said Billy. He closed the book and took it into the house.

The old hounds, Drum and Major, went running out. Yes, it was Pappy. The team splashed through the ford, came part way up the barn road and stopped. The wagon was empty of logs now, but carried several sacks of wheat flour and a supply of feed. And there at Pappy's feet in front sat a new hound dog—a puppy. Drum and Major began to growl.

Mammy looked on and didn't say a word. Pappy handed the flour sacks down to Billy and talked loudly.

"Stone Mountain's a tough little ole hill to haul over," he said. "I most got drownded over there in Tennessee. Water was mighty high on the way back. When we forded Forge Creek, hit carried me and the horses down a fur piece. Lucky some Tennessee feller come along just then with a yoke o' oxen and pulled us out."

Billy stared at the hound pup. He didn't know what to think. He didn't know whether to be glad or sad.

"Where'd you get the pup, Pappy?" he asked. He patted it on the head.

"Oh, that critter!" Pappy laughed. "Got him off Walt Moseley. He's a born possum dog, I can tell by the look of him."

"We got plenty good-for-nothin' hounds already," said Mammy. "There's a heap o' things we need more'n new hound dogs. You're gettin' to be as bad as that low-down Pappy Weaselface—he'd give his last shirt for another huntin' dog."

"Now, Ruthie," said Pappy, "you said you was tired o' havin' them possums steal all your young chickens."

"He's only a pup," said Mammy. "Precious lot of possums he'll catch."

"He'll be a right smart possum dog come fall," said Pappy.

The pup followed Billy up the steps and into the house. In the kitchen Mammy shook the ashes down in the step-stove, got the fire going and lifted the cloth that covered the food still sitting on the table.

Billy took his dulcimer from the fireboard in the front room and sat down on a chair, with the new hound pup at his feet. A small fire was burning in the fireplace. He began to strum the dulcimer with the noter. His mind was made up. The wish-book had decided the matter. He didn't like the way Jeb Dotson had acted about his trading. He wouldn't buy the second-hand banjo from Jeb after all. He'd choose a new one from the mail-order catalogue and send away for it. He began to sing softly:

> "Whet up your knife and whistle up your dog,
> Whet up your knife and whistle up your dog,
> We're going to the holler to catch a ground hog,
> Ground hog!

> Too many rocks and too many logs,
> Too many rocks and too many logs,
> Too many rocks to hunt ground hogs,
> Ground hogs!

Over the hills and through the bresh,
Over the hills and through the bresh,
There we struck that hog-sign fresh,
                    Sign fresh!

Two in the clift and one in the log,
Two in the clift and one in the log,
I saw his nose and I knew he was a hog,
                    Was a hog. . . ."

After unhitching the horses at the barn, Pappy came in through the kitchen, but he did not stop to eat. He came straight into the front room to see where the music was coming from. He planted his two feet wide apart and looked at Billy, astonished.

"So this is what's been goin' on while I been gone," he said.

Letty Jo and the little ones came out of the bedroom.

"Bill, what you think you're doin'?" asked Pappy.

The boy jumped to his feet and hung his head. Pap's voice sounded very cross and made him feel guilty. He thought quickly and could not remember any wrong he had done. He started to speak, but could not think what to say.

"What's that ere thing you're a-holdin' in your hand?" demanded Pappy.

"Hit's . . . hit's a dulci-more."

"Who does hit belong to? Uncle Pozy?" demanded Pappy.

"No, hit's . . . hit's mine," answered Billy. "I made it. Uncle Pozy helped. He showed me how."

"Now, Rudy, don't you go pesterin' the boy," said Mammy,

[ 127 ]

looking in from the kitchen. "He's been workin' so hard all spring, I 'lowed he could go over to Uncle Pozy's and pleasure himself a bit, and he was takened with the i-dee he'd like a dulci-more. . . ."

"Fool business!" cried Pappy angrily. "Fine way to carry on while I'm gone, when I told him to tarry at home and tend to weedin' and hoein' the crops." He looked at his wife. "The Bronson music comin' out, I s'pose. He's gonna be like them shiftless brothers and nephews o' your'n, who druther play and sing than dig and hoe."

"Where's the harm in playin' and singin'?" asked Mammy.

"I never seen a good fiddler or banjo picker that was worth his salt for anything else," said Pappy. "Fiddlers are not even worth shootin'. There's that brother Jamie o' your'n—he'll sit and fiddle and pat his foot and forget to put in his crops. Is that the way you're raisin' up this boy?"

"None of the Bronsons has starved yet," Mammy held up her chin, "and they all know how to get a little joy out o' life. There ain't no harm in a little music, if hit pleaures the boy to make it. Hit keeps us from gettin' lonesome up here in this dark valley, when we're all alone by ourselves. Billy's that bright and gaily, I miss him when he goes off anywheres, but you can't keep a boy tied up like a dog."

"Goin' off somewheres," said Pappy. "He's good at that. Always traipsin' and gallivantin' away from work. Goin' to Uncle Pozy's, goin' to Uncle Jamie's, goin' to mill, goin' a-roamin', goin' to Jeb Dotson's store. . . . Yes, I heard you been down there." He glared at the boy.

Mammy came in and wiped her hands on her apron.

"If you don't like the way I'm raisin' the boy, Rudy, you'd better bide home and raise him yourself," she said.

"How can I bide home when I'm loggin'? Why should I bide home when I got a wife and young uns, and a son most growed to look after the crops?"

"He's only ten, Rudy," said Mammy, "though he looks like a little ole man already, the way he's been worked. Hit'll be many a day afore he's growed."

"Think money grows on bushes, don't you?" Pappy went on. "Work never stunted a young un yet." He turned sharply to the boy. "Did you get them beans hoed, like I told you, son?"

"No sir," faltered Billy, "I didn't know just when you was a-comin' home and——"

"Hand me over that ere dulci-more," said his father in a quiet voice.

Billy clutched it tighter and looked up with pleading eyes. Mammy and Letty Jo and the little redheads stared. They all loved the tune-box that Billy had made, but they couldn't say anything. Billy stood still. Surely Pappy wouldn't take it from him.

But Pappy did. He seized the dulcimer and threw it into the open fireplace. He found some kindling and started a blaze.

Billy looked on. His face turned white, but he made no

sound. No sign of emotion betrayed the turmoil of his feelings.

Red Top and Mazie ran over to watch the dulcimer burn. Mammy took one look at the stricken boy and went back to the kitchen.

"Music won't grow corn and beans," said Pappy in a low, meaningful voice. Then he went out to get his supper.

Billy knew the dulcimer would never be mentioned again. What was settled, was settled. That was Pap's way. The boy sat down on his chair, his arms hanging limply at his sides, his eyes on the fire. He felt as if a part of himself were being destroyed, and he had no more strength left in him.

Letty Jo suddenly burst out crying.

"Hush up!" called Pappy, from the kitchen.

Letty Jo hushed. The little ones forgot the dulcimer and began to play with the new pup.

Billy could hear his father's voice demanding food: "Corn-bread." He knew his mother was waiting on him. After a while, "Beans." "More beans." "Biscuit. Where's the biscuit-bread?" "Well, I brung you plenty white flour, now you can make biscuits again." Then, "Corn-bread."

Not a word from Mammy.

Then an angry shout: "Ain't that sorry, good-for-nothin' boy keepin' the water-bucket full? Bill! Bill Honeycutt!"

Billy ran out.

"Go to the spring and fill that bucket for your Mammy. Hain't I told you to keep it full?"

[ 130 ]

Billy took the cedar bucket and ran out the back door to the branch. He skipped over the plank, dipped the bucket into the pool at the spring and filled it.

When he got back to the house, his father was standing at the door. He took the bucket from him, dashed the water on the ground, and handed it back to the boy without a word.

Billy didn't know what to think. He walked slowly to the spring and filled the bucket again. When he brought it back to the door, his father dashed the water on the ground the second time.

Five times he filled it, and each time his father emptied it. Billy knew now that he was being punished.

The sixth time his father poured the water into his mother's dishpan, and the seventh into one of the milk-piggins. It took a great many buckets of water to fill all the receptacles in the house, including the two washtubs. It took so many, Billy lost count.

He was very tired when, at last, his father set the final bucket of water on the kitchen table, dipped the gourd dipper in it, and drank.

The boy was thirsty too, but he did not ask for a drink.

"That'll learn you to keep your Mammy's water bucket filled," said Pappy in a low tone, "and hit'll learn you who's boss in this house." He lifted his foot and

[ 132 ]

gave the boy a kick. "Now, git yourself to bed!"

Billy climbed wearily up to the loft, sick at heart.

The next morning he woke early. It was hardly light when he crept down the stairs, past the bedroom where his father lay snoring, and out the back door. He jumped on Old Bet and rode as fast as he could down Roundabout Creek.

Before he reached the Turn-Off, he heard hoofbeats. Wondering who might be out so early, he pulled the mule up and waited under an overhanging tree. Out from the Turn-Off came a spotted horse and a skinny black horse. The men riding were Walt Moseley and Pappy Weaselface. They were riding silently, without saying a word.

Billy waited until they had been gone a long time, then he started on again and rode to Jeb Dotson's store. Dawn glowed pink over Solitude as he rode up.

Jeb Dotson was still in bed. Billy rattled the store door, then rode round to the bedroom window and pounded on it. Jeb had his windows barred with heavy iron gratings. Jeb knew well the tricks of mischievous boys, and was anxious to protect his store and its contents from the damage and breakage of possible marauders.

He raised himself up on one elbow and, wild-eyed and tousle-headed, stared out through the unwashed glass window.

"Unlock the door!" called Billy Honeycutt. He spoke calmly, though he was burning up with excitement inside.

"I'll hand over all the money I got," Jeb called in a frightened voice, "if you'll promise not to shoot."

"I won't shoot," answered Billy. "Unlock the door."

By the time Jeb reached the door and unlocked it, he had had time to think. "You're just a bunch o' sorry old gamesome boys!" he yelled. "What you want?"

"Unlock the door, I said!" called Billy.

With trembling hands, Jeb Dotson put his key in the padlock and turned it. He removed the lock and slowly opened the door. He stood in his nightshirt and peered out. He saw Billy Honeycutt but no one else.

"Where's the others, Bill?" Jeb whispered.

"Hidin' round the corner," answered the boy.

Jeb opened the door a little wider. "What you want, Bill?"

Billy jumped off the mule and pushed the man aside. He stared into the dusky darkness but saw no baskets there. Not a single basket of his or Uncle Pozy's hung where they had hung before. They must have been sold. A wave of happiness swept over him. The loss of the dulcimer was nothing. Soon he'd have his banjo.

"What you mean, a-wakin' a man out of his sleep in the middle of the night? What you want, so soon of a mornin'?" asked Jeb.

"I want my money."

"What money, Bill?" Jeb scratched his head.

"The money for them baskets I brung you," said Billy. "You sold 'em, didn't you?"

"Yep, that Miz Sutherland from Asheville bought 'em as

[ 134 ]

soon as you left that day," said Jeb. "That was what she was settin' round here so long for—makin' up her mind. She's takin' 'em to some place down the country to sell 'em again to city folks. She bought all Uncle Pozy's too. I packed 'em up and had 'em hauled to the depot at Cranberry, to be shipped to her."

"She paid money for 'em too, didn't she?" demanded Billy.

"I reckon she did," admitted Jeb.

"And you gave me credit."

"I reckon," said Jeb, "but I don't recollect——"

"You totted it down in your book," said Billy. "Go, look-see how much."

Jeb scratched his head again. "Hit's done took off the book," he said, "'cause the transaction's ended. The trade's over."

"What you mean—the trade's over?"

Jeb began to feel uncomfortable under the boy's stern gaze. Bill Honeycutt was growing up. He couldn't be trifled with. Jeb was in a predicament and didn't well know how to get out of it.

"Get my money, Jeb," said Billy, "or I'll call them Buckwheat Holler boys and we'll come in and help ourselves and mess up your store."

"Gosh almighty, don't do that, keep them gamesome boys away!" wailed Jeb. He began to tremble. "I can't give it to you, 'cause I hain't got nary a penny of it."

"What you done with hit?" asked Billy. "You ain't losted it? Hit ain't been stole? You said as hit would be safe with you."

"Your Pap . . . your Pap——"

"You hain't give hit to Pappy?" cried Billy in anger and alarm. "I told you this here was my own trade and not my Mammy's or Pappy's."

"You said your Mammy wasn't cravin' sugar and coffee, as I recollect hit," said Jeb. "I asked you if your Pappy knowed about this deal o' your'n and you said he didn't. So I thought hit my bounden duty to tell him about hit, and hit made him mighty cranky, hearin' you was sellin' baskets to put Uncle Pozy out o' business. When I told him you was fixin' to buy that second-hand banjo of Old Mack Muller's, he got rarin' mad."

Billy stopped to think. So Pappy had known all about it.

[ 136 ]

That was why he was so cross last night, burned the dulcimer and made him carry all that water. Billy's heart sank, but not for long.

"I ain't buyin' no second-hand banjo offen you, Jeb Dotson," he said.

"Not good enough, eh?" sneered Jeb. "Well, you won't be buyin' none at all, that's sure as the graveyard!"

"Where's my money?" demanded Billy, suddenly panic-stricken.

"Your Pap bought a hound pup with it," said Jeb. He smiled broadly as if it were a grand joke.

Billy's mouth fell open in surprise. Then he recovered.

"No, he didn't," he told Jeb. "He swapped Walt Moseley for that pup. He said so, and my Pap don't tell lies."

"Hit was this way:" said Jeb, "Walt Moseley and Pappy Weaselface and some other fellers was tryin' to see whose hound dog was the best fighter. So they lined up all their hounds here in front of the store one day, and turned an old tom cat loose. All the dogs turned tail and run, but that little pup o' Walt's. He licked the daylights out of the tom cat. So everybody said that the pup was the fightingest hound in the county. Walt said he come of a possum-dog breed and could smell a possum a mile off. Your Pap said there wasn't nothin' he wanted more'n a good possum dog, so———"

"What did he swap for the pup?" asked Billy.

"Er . . . what?"

"What did Pap give Walt for that pup?" asked Billy again.

[ 137 ]

Jeb Dotson scratched his head and said, "I done told you before."

"What?"

"He said you was too young to go tradin' around for yourself, so your money rightly belonged to him. What you earn until you're twenty-one is your Pap's—don't you know that? He told me to hand the money over, so there wasn't nothin' else I could do. He didn't make a swap, he *bought* that pup."

Still Billy could not believe it.

"What did Pap give for that hound pup?" he asked again. *"Your money!"*

Jeb shouted the two words, shut the door quickly and snapped the padlock.

## CHAPTER X

## *Old-timey Chimney*

BILLY couldn't bear to look at the hound pup for a long time. He tried to shut it out of the house. He refused to feed it. He kicked it with his bare foot every chance he got. He hated seeing it around, because it was a constant reminder of his loss.

The day Pappy named the pup "Banjo," Billy went off roaming in the woods and didn't come back until nightfall.

But there was nothing he could do about it. Banjo stayed and became one of the family. Pappy bragged about Banjo, and said he was getting bigger and smarter every day. Still Billy could not look at him.

But the time came when the boy's troubles were swallowed up in a greater calamity, and he had to forget himself. Warm summer weather had come quickly as it does in the mountains. One day Billy heard surprising news. Pappy was telling it to Mammy.

"I stopped to see the high-sheriff again," said Pappy, "and he says I can turn them Trivetts out of that shack up on the mountain. The surveyor's been here and says all that land up there is set down in my deed. Hit belongs to me, so now I can get shet of that troublesome pair. I won't law 'em for trespassin'. I'll just dispossess 'em, move 'em out."

"Where will they go, Rudy?" asked Mammy in a low voice.

"To their kinfolks, I reckon."

"Down the country?" asked Mammy. "You can't transplant old Gran no more'n you can that big cowcumber tree, you know that, Rudy."

"That's their business," said Pappy.

"So that was the surveyor that day," said Mammy, "that fat feller with the possumy grin on his face."

"He said he come while I was on one of my jaunts to Mountain City," said Pappy.

"Yes, he come here and scared me half to death, after goin' up to Gran's and scarin' the life out o' her. We thought he was the high-sheriff," said Mammy.

"Why, he's a right nice-lookin' feller," said Pap, smiling. "Nothin' scary-lookin' about him."

Pappy sat down on a chair and tried to be agreeable.

"The high-sheriff advised me against turning the Trivetts out by force," he said. "Advised more peaceable ways. Now,

[ 140 ]

Ruthie, I want you to do somethin' for me—go up and see old Granny and try to argify her peaceable-like to go and live with some of her kin. I'll be willing to carry all her plunder in my jolt-wagon, even if I have to go clean to the level lands with it . . ."

"Rudolphus Honeycutt!" cried Mammy, her eyes ablaze. "You are a low-down wretch!"

Pappy saw there was no use trying to be tactful any longer. Besides, he was angry.

"Either you go do what I say," he said in a low tone, "or I'll *down* that cowcumber tree this day." He got up and went out.

Mammy was always quiet, obedient and soft-spoken. But now she too was angry. "I'll wait on you hand and foot, Rudy

Honeycutt, to my dyin' day, as a dutiful wife is bound to do," she called after him, "but I'll be horn-swoggled if you can scare me with your wicked threats." Then she added: "You don't *want* the high-sheriff comin' round here, do you, Rudy? You don't *want* him to see what's goin' on, on yon side of Laurel Mountain, do you?"

Pappy did not answer.

"The crops need tendin', Rudy." Mammy stood on the back porch and made one final appeal. "Stay home and make the crops, Rudy, so we can eat hearty come winter."

Pappy stopped in his tracks to answer back: "What have I got me a wife and young uns and a son almost growed for, if not to tend the crops? I'm a hunter and a horse-swapper and a logger—not a farmer."

He went to the barn to get his logging chains and started off with the team. Billy and Mammy watched him go, splashing through the ford.

"You go up the trail, son," said Mammy. "If he starts to saw down that cowcumber tree, come and tell me. No—maybe you'd better go warn Granny first. Tell her your Pap's comin' to throw her out, and if he does, she's to come here."

"Here, Mammy?" cried Billy, astonished. "What will Pap say to that?"

"Never mind, son. You go do as I bid you."

Billy climbed the trail to the Half-Way-Up House.

"Hello! Hello, Granny! Hello!" he called.

He paused, hearing a voice. Sarey Sue was singing:

[ 142 ]

"Oh, fly around, my pretty little miss
    Fly around, my daisy;
Fly around, my pretty little miss,
    You almost drive me crazy.

Her cheeks as red as a red, red rose,
    Her eyes as a diamond brown;
I'm goin' to see my pretty little miss,
    Before the sun goes down.

Every time I go that road,
    It looks so dark and cloudy,
Every time I see that girl
    I always tell her *howdy.* . . ."

The song trailed off and Billy could hear the girl talking. He called again. Sarey Sue came out on the porch.

"Where's Granny?"

"Out somewheres," said Sarey Sue, nodding vaguely.

"Who was you a-talkin' to in there?" asked Billy.

"Only myself," giggled Sarey Sue. "When I'm by myself, I talk to myself just like as if I had somebody there to talk to."

Billy stared at the girl. "Law sakes! What a sight!" he exclaimed. "You're a sight on earth!"

"Who? Me?"

"Yes, you."

Sarey Sue was indeed a sight. Her face, arms and legs were covered with soot.

"What's happened?" demanded Billy.

"That blame chimney keeps a-fallin' down," said Sarey Sue.

[ 143 ]

"Hit's an ole-timey one and we never know when the rocks will fall. I was tryin' to be real careful, so I made a little bitty oak fire to get my breakfast—Gran, she et some corn-bread and left afore sun-up. So I takes my case knife and leans down to turn my meat in the fryin' pan on the coals, and *wham!* If a big rock don't fall plumb on my hand and make a big lump and a bruise." She held out her hand. "Hit's a sight! I jumped back just in time, for more rocks come bouncin' down right on. . . ."

"You're the smuttiest person ever I did see," said Billy. He went in the house and looked up the chimney. "Reckon I'll have to tote them rocks out o' the fireplace for you," he added, "or you can't cook no more vittles."

"You'll be a sight, too!" laughed Sarey Sue.

"You ain't told me where Gran is," said Billy, carrying rocks out the back door. "She ain't gone clear over to Three Top to tend Liza Moseley, has she?"

Sarey Sue shook her head. "Sereny Holbrook's ailin' and 'lowed she needed a tonic, so Gran brewed her some bitters out o' wild cherry bark and sassyfrack and takened it down to her. Then she come back home and——"

"Where's she at *now?*" Billy remembered his errand.

"Out somewheres," said Sarey Sue, waving her blackened arm. "She's just like a butterfly, here and yonder where there's anything to git."

"What's she after?"

"If hit ain't yarbs, hit's berries," said Sarey Sue. "She's a

[ 144 ]

regular berry picker—strawberries, poke berries, huckleberries, but just now, hit's blackberries she's after—gonna dry 'em for winter. Some folks *dig* blackberry roots to sell, but we don't. We want the berries on 'em." Sarey Sue smiled with pride. "Law, Granny'll pick fifty gallons of 'em before she's done. I can't never keep her in her chair, she just won't stay sot."

Billy brought another load of stones out.

"But whereabouts *is* she?" he asked.

"Lordy mercy!" Sarey Sue threw up her hands. "How should I know? She might be on Three Top, she might be on the Peak . . . she might be anywheres."

Billy looked up at the chimney again. "Hit ain't safe," he said. "This house ain't fitten for you folkses to live in. Maybe Pap's right." He remembered Mammy's message, but how could he break the news to Sarey Sue, so gay and cheerful?

"I got somethin' to show you," said Sarey Sue. She ran to a pile of quilts stacked on the chest by the loom. She pulled off the top one.

"What's that?" asked Billy.

"Hit's a new quilt-top I pieced up," said Sarey Sue, filled with pride. "I'm good at finger-sewin'. I make Granny's aprons and sew pockets on 'em too. Looky! See all them nice, even, teeny-tiny stitches?"

Billy took one look and started to go.

"I had a dream last night," Sarey Sue went on gaily. "I was

sleepin' under my quilt-top for the first time. Know what they say about that? Your dream'll come *true!* Guess what my dream was. Hit was about *you!*"

Billy went right on walking out the door. He had wasted a lot of time and he must find Granny and tell her.

"I dreamed you had a fotched-on fiddle——"

The boy turned and glared at her. "Ain't I told you——"

"And you went to the Fiddlers' Convention," Sarey Sue went on, "and took first prize you played so good. You was the Champion Fiddler of the County—but that wasn't all. After that, you was the Champion Fiddler of North Caroliny, and better than that, you got to be Champion Fiddler of the whole U. S. Nation!"

The boy stood still, his back turned, and said not a word.

"I believe in dreams, don't you?" Sarey Sue's voice sounded so bright and happy. "When a girl sleeps under a quilt for the first time, her dream's *obliged* to come true, ain't hit?"

Billy clenched his fists at his side. He turned his head and spoke bitterly. "Pap burnt my dulci-more in the fire, and he took my banjo money and bought a hound pup with it!" He blurted out the words. Sarey Sue might as well know the truth and forget her silly dreams. "How could I ever get to be a Champion music-player?"

"Oh!" said Sarey Sue, in a sharp cry of pain. "I didn't know. . . . How could he be so mean? How could he? I wouldn't take that offen him, if he was my Pappy."

Billy turned his back again and gulped. "When hit's your own Pap, you take hit," he said. "No, he ain't mean. He just says music don't grow corn and beans, and I reckon hit don't. He says he don't want no little ole timidy men around, and he's raisin' me up to be tough. . . ."

"But oh, I *do* believe in dreams, don't you?" cried Sarey Sue. Her voice was filled with sadness, but it had not lost hope. Then she burst out crying: "I'm goin' right on believin' hit. . . ."

Billy understood how the girl felt. She had nothing—only dreams to believe in. When you had nothing at all, you could have everything in dreams . . . even if they never came true. But he could not find the words to say this to Sarey Sue.

"I got to find your Gran," said Billy, starting off. "I got bad news for her."

[ 147 ]

"Bad news?" Sarey Sue stared. "Why didn't you say so? I'll go along. You'd never find her."

It wasn't as hard to find her as they thought it would be. They started back up the mountain and heard voices. The voices led them to the cowcumber tree on the ridge. The air was bright and clear today, and the far-off mountains were cut sharply in a pattern of deep blue.

Billy was too late with his warning. Granny Trivett was not picking blackberries, she was talking to Billy's father and Ollie Holbrook. She looked like a statue. She was standing in front of the big tree, her thin old arms outspread to protect it.

"Ye'll cut it down, Rudy Honeycutt, over my dead body." Her voice was firm and low, without a tremor in it.

"This is my land," answered Pappy. "I'll cut what trees I please."

"Hit ain't your land," insisted Granny. "Hit belonged first to my Great-Granpap Goforth and he handed it down to me. I got a paper with writin' on, to prove hit."

"Where's your paper?" asked Ollie Holbrook. "Maybe she's right, Rudy."

"Where's your paper?" demanded Honeycutt.

Granny hesitated. "I can't seem to recollect . . ." Her voice grew vague. "I put hit somewheres. . . ."

"Well, *my* paper, down to the Court house," Rudy Honeycutt pulled the copy out of his pocket and read aloud: "says my line runs along the ridge 'westward to a poplar tree and then to an old fence row at an agreed corner . . .' so this is *my* tree and I'll chop hit down whenever I'm a mind to."

"A cowcumber tree ain't a poplar, Rudy. A tulip tree's sometimes called a yellow poplar, but not a cowcumber." Ollie Holbrook's voice was patient. "And 'to an old fence row at an agreed corner'—that ain't what you'd call precise."

"This is the oldest tree on the ridge," said Rudy. "Hit's the only tree that could a been standin' when this deed was writ."

"That air a true word," said Ollie.

"But a cowcumber ain't a poplar," interrupted Granny. "Any old fool knows that."

"She'll stand there all day, Rudy," said Ollie in a low voice. "Don't see how we can saw the tree down as long as she's there."

Rudy hated to admit defeat. Without saying more to the old woman, he began to gather up his axe, crosscut saw and chains. Then he saw Billy, with black-faced Sarey Sue beside him. "What you doin' here, son?" he growled.

"Mammy told me to come," answered Billy. "She told me to run tell her quick when you begun to notch the tree."

"She did, eh?"

Pappy walked on with Ollie Holbrook and soon the two disappeared in the brush.

"Reckon they're a-goin' to the still?" whispered Sarey Sue.

"What still?" Granny's voice was sharp.

"They're headin' for No Man's Cove," insisted the girl. "Hit's right down yonder, below the cowcumber tree."

"Sarey Sue!" scolded Granny. "How often do I got to tell you to keep your mouth shut and mind your own business?"

Billy glared at the girl. She was so dumb sometimes. "My Pap ain't runnin' no still," he said angrily. "He's gone off that-a-way just to cover his tracks. He's really headin' for . . ." How could he tell Granny his own Pap was going to run her out of her home? He paused, then added lamely, "You'd better hurry home quick!"

"Oh Gran, did you see them big blackberries we passed on the way up?" cried Sarey Sue. "Right there by that slick old rock?"

"Granny," Billy began again, "if Pap comes . . . Mammy said if Pap comes to your house . . . and tries to start somethin'——"

[ 150 ]

"Why, your Pap won't have no leg left to stand on," laughed Granny. "I ain't afeared one mite."

Billy shook his head. Granny refused to see danger even when it was coming straight at her. They walked leisurely down the mountain, picking blackberries along the trail. Billy picked with them. Granny insisted on filling her two buckets. Sarey Sue made a gay story about the chimney falling down, and told how Billy took the rocks out.

When they reached the cabin, they saw a horse hitched to a land sled, standing at the foot of the porch. On the sled were loaded the spool bed, the bureau and the two chairs. Ollie Holbrook and Rudy Honeycutt were carrying bedding and kitchen utensils out of the house.

Granny Trivett set her berries down, then stood still and stared, unable to say a word. Billy stared too. Pap meant what he said, after all. He was moving the Trivetts out.

"What you doin', you two?" screamed Sarey Sue, rushing up and shaking her fists at the men. "Settin' us out in the road? Where can we go? Where can we go?"

"Hush up, gal young un," said Granny.

"You can go to your kinfolks," said Pappy in a loud voice.

Then Billy remembered what Mammy had told him to say. He whispered something in Granny's ear.

"Yes, son," said Granny. "That's a good i-dee. But first, I'm fixin' to go in my house and git somethin'. Them stones fallin' down in that old-timey chimney made me recollect . . ."

When she came out, she had one apron pocket well padded

and two strong safety-pins holding it shut. Sarey Sue brought her accordion and hugged it close. Without a word to the two men, Granny went with Billy down the trail, while Sarey Sue followed at their heels.

Mammy met Granny at the door, found her a chair and put chicken on the kitchen stove to fry. Then she heated a tub of water, so Sarey Sue could take a bath and wash the soot off.

"What with all the work of keepin' one's soul alive," said Granny, "a body don't have much time for neighborin'."

"You said a true word," replied Mammy. "You're welcome, Granny, you and Sarey Sue, to stay as long as you're a mind to. I'll fix up your bed in the parlor."

"In the parlor?" cackled Granny, with a twinkle in her eye. "Lordy mercy, Ruthie, I never knowed you-uns was fine folks!"

Sarey Sue insisted on being shown all over the house, as if she had never been inside before. She touched everything in every room, asking, "Whose is this?" until Letty Jo got tired of answering her, and said, "It just belongs to the family."

"Bless goodness!" said Sarey Sue, with a restful sigh.

The new arrivals made themselves at home quickly.

"Let me help you string them beans, Ruthie, and cut up them punkins," said Granny, "so you can get 'em dried for winter." With a large darning needle, she began to string the bean pods on a long string.

Sarey Sue played her gayest tune on her dead Pappy's accordion, while Billy watched and listened.

When Pappy brought the sled-load of furniture down, he stopped by the door and came marching into the kitchen. "Where's Gran goin'?" he asked Mammy. "Where do I haul her plunder to?"

"Take hit around to the front door," said Mammy. "They're stayin' here, Granny and Sarey Sue. I'm makin' up their bed in the parlor."

Pappy's mouth fell open. "What did you say?"

"They're fixin' to stay till you mend their chimney, Rudy," said Mammy. "Hit ain't safe, with rocks fallin' down every day. That ole cabin ain't fitten for a chicken to live in. Roof leaks too—you'll have to get Uncle Pozy to rive 'em some clapboards for a new roof."

"I told 'em to go to their kinfolks," said Pappy, frowning.

"They ain't got no kin but us," said Mammy, with a gleam of triumph in her eye. "Them that sets traps sometimes goes and puts their foot in 'em."

There was no answer to that. There was nothing for Pappy to do but let them stay.

But he did not like it. He hated Granny's cackle and her everlasting chatter. He disliked Sarey Sue's giggle and the

[ 154 ]

noisy clamor of her accordion, which she played any time, day or night. It was bad enough when they were all over the mountain, but it was still worse to have them all over his own house.

"They got to get out o' here!" Pappy said at last. "I'll take 'em anywheres!"

"You don't have to go far," said Mammy, with a smile. "All they want is to go half-way back up the mountain."

"Then why don't they go?"

"Granny won't go till you look at that paper of her Granpap's," said Mammy. "She had it hid behind a stone in that ole-timey chimney, and forgot hit. When the rocks fell out, she found hit again."

"Fiddlesticks! I'll give her the house and the cowcumber tree and the whole mountain, if she'll go and take that gal young un with that ear-bustin' cantrapshun away from here," threatened Pappy.

"You won't give 'em to her," said Mammy. "They're hers already."

Pappy looked at Granny's paper, and when he handed it back, he said, "All right. I'll mend the chimney and fix the roof. Get 'em out of here."

The very next day the Trivetts moved home again.

CHAPTER XI

## The Cry of a Panther

"I see my mule a-comin'
He's a-comin' with a smile;
If you don't watch out
He'll kick you half a mile . . ."

WHOA mule! Whoa, I say! Ary letter for me, Miss Viney?"

Old Bet was getting older and bonier, and Billy's long legs seemed to almost touch the ground, as he leaned over and put his head in at the post-office door.

As usual, the postmistress shook her head. "Who'd be a-writin' to you, Billy Honeycutt?"

"Dunno . . . but the mail-wagon's always bringin' the mail-bag over from the depot, with letters in hit, and——"

"Go 'long with you now. Shoo!" Miss Viney lifted her

broom to chase him from the door.

"Hi, there, son!" called a hearty voice. "Where you been a-keepin' yourself?"

There in the road stood Uncle Pozy with a load of baskets. He was on his way to Jeb Dotson's store. All summer long, Billy had never once gone to see him, and had purposely avoided him. Now he could not escape.

"How be ye, son?" asked the old man.

"Common," grunted Billy.

"You ain't been to see me lately, son."

"No, sir," said Billy. "Right smart o' work to do at home."

"Sold all your baskets, didn't ye, son? And so did I. Mighty lucky, wasn't we, to find such a good customer? Did Jeb tell you about Miz Lucy Sutherland who bought 'em all and paid money for 'em?"

Billy hung his head and did not reply.

"I reckoned you'd come over right soon after that," Uncle Pozy went on, "to make a heap more. See how many I've made? But you never come. I been hankerin' for you, son. Livin' all alone like I do, I kinda craved your company. . . ."

"I ain't makin' no more baskets," said Billy bluntly

Uncle Pozy pondered the boy's reply but did not question it.

"Likely you've been practisin' on your dulci-more," he said, smiling. "Like as not you're so busy makin' purty music, ye ain't got time to make old ugly baskets. . . ."

Then it came out. "Don't never want to see nary dulci-more again, long as I live!"

"What you done with hit, son?" asked Uncle Pozy, startled.

"Pap burnt hit up in the fire first day he seen it," the boy blurted out. "Ain't had none the whole endurin' summer."

"Shoo, now!" Uncle Pozy's voice was full of sympathy. "Ain't that just too bad. But you come from a tune-makin' family, Billy. All your Mammy's folks can sing and play, and you got the knack for it, I can tell. Your Pap ought to sense that. Hit ain't somethin' he can step on and stamp out. Hit's there and hit's bound to grow. Course I don't want to set you agin your Pappy. . . . Why, there's your Mammy's brother, Fiddlin' Jamie, the best fiddler in the mountains, a singin' fiddler too. . . ." Uncle Pozy paused.

"Would hit pleasure you to come and spend the day with me," he asked, "and make you another dulci-more, son?"

"Never want to see none again, long as I live!" repeated Billy.

[ 158 ]

"Would hit pleasure you to play on *my* dulci-more now and again?"

"Never want to see nary dulci-more again, I said."

Uncle Pozy pondered. He could see that the boy had been deeply hurt.

"Do you see them cousins o' yours in Last Hope Holler sometimes?" he asked.

"Pappy says they're sorry old boys——" began Billy.

"But your Mammy lets you go spend the day with 'em now and again, 'cause they're your kinfolks, don't she?"

"Law, yes," admitted Billy.

"They're as fine a batch o' boys as ever I see," said Uncle Pozy. "Good workers, but ready for a bit o' fun, too. Hit pleasures you to go visit 'em, don't hit?

"Law, yes," said Billy, smiling feebly.

Uncle Pozy turned to go to the store. Billy gave Old Bet a slap on the rump and started off.

"Your Uncle Jamie's got a mighty fine fiddle!" Uncle Pozy shouted loudly so Billy could hear it over the clop-clop of the little gray mule's hoofs. *"A mighty fine fiddle . . . a mighty fine fiddle . . ."* the words seemed to sing themselves over and over again, as Old Bet trotted along.

He hadn't told Uncle Pozy, but he was on his way to Uncle Jamie's in Last Hope Hollow. He'd worked hard, helping cut the hay and stack it in the pastures, and fence the stacks in. He'd hoed corn all summer till it was laid by, and after that, pulled fodder for days. So when Pappy went off to the county seat, Mammy said he deserved a rest and sent him to Uncle

Jamie's. He was to spend the night too.

The boys were out when he got there, so he sat down in the front room and had a good visit with Uncle Jamie and Aunt Tallie and Ettie Bell. After they had talked a while, Uncle Jamie took down his fiddle and began to play. Billy forgot everything else as he listened.

"Want to try hit, Bill?" Uncle Jamie handed over the fiddle and bow. "Not one of them boys o' mine takes to hit. You can lead a horse to water, but you can't make him play the fiddle."

It was very different from the dulcimer, but Billy hadn't watched Fiddlin' Jamie all his life for nothing. He liked the feel of the fiddle under his chin and the bow in his hands. With a few instructions from his uncle, he was soon playing a passable tune.

"Not bad, not bad!" said Uncle Jamie, in great excitement. "Shake hit out, boy, shake hit out! Ruthie's boy will be a fiddler yet. Won't she be the plumb tickledest woman in the mountains! I'll tell you what I want you to do, Bill. You come over whenever you can and soon I'll have you rattlin' some bang-up tunes outa that little ole fiddle o' mine. You've got the knack, Lord love ye!"

Glen and Jack came tearing in, with Rick not far behind them. "Have you heard the news?" they cried.

"What news?" asked Billy.

"There's a panther loose in the mountains!" He pronounced the word "painter."

Uncle Jamie threw back his head and laughed.

"You needn't laugh, Pap!" said Rick. "Hit's been seen on Phoenix Mountain."

"Hit killed a pig on Jeff Allison's farm and two sheep in Harm Higgins' pasture," said Glen, his eyes bulging.

"And Lem Bowlin seen it today on his way to Wiley's mill," added Jack.

"Golly!" cried Billy. "Right here on Little Laurel Creek?"

"Yep," said Rick. "Guess what I'm fixin' to do. I'm goin' out tonight and ketch that ere painter."

The boys looked at each other. "We'll all go," they said.

"Go ahead!" laughed Uncle Jamie. "You're only young once!"

"We'll camp on the mountain all night," said Jack.

Aunt Tallie had a good supper as she always did, and afterwards, the boys began their preparations. They put corn-bread and biscuits in a sack and got two guns, but decided that blankets were too heavy to carry. They put oil in the lantern. The dogs came running, all four of them—Troop, Nip, Punch and Gum.

"We'll take the hounds," said Rick. "Old Gum too—he's part bull-dog—for protection."

"There's a big rock-cave up on Laurel Mountain," said Jack, as they started out. "The painter might be denning in there."

"We'd ought to go where the varmint's been seen," said Rick. "We'll go by Wiley's mill first, then cut across Harm Higgins' pasture and come up around Jeff Allison's farm."

"Then if the dogs don't get no scent, we can go on up to the cave," said Jack.

The boys agreed. They followed Little Laurel Creek till they came to Wiley's mill. The sun had just gone down over the mountain, and the little valley was bathed in a soft purple glow. The boys listened carefully, but there was no noise except the rushing of water over the water wheel.

"Painters prowl when they're hungry," said Glen, "mostly early morning and right after sundown. This is just the time for 'em to be out."

Lee Wiley's house looked quiet and peaceful beside the mill. The boys saw his wife go in the back door carrying two buckets of milk.

"Aw, this ain't no fun," complained Jack, "a-huntin' a painter when there ain't none. Pap said the painters was all killed out forty years ago."

"Not *all!*" protested Rick. "Lem Bowlin said he seen one *today.*"

They followed a winding dirt road which curled around and up the side of Ivy Mountain. All the way to Harm Higgins' place, which was perched like a bird's nest on the steep slope, the boys grew more doubtful of the panther's existence.

"I tell you what let's do," suggested Rick. "Let's make out like there *is* a painter loose, and see if we can scare folks."

The boys agreed this would be fun.

"You do the squealing, Rick," said Billy. "You got the singingest voice. I recollect how you called them quail that time and they come up and walked all over you. Likely you can make a noise like a painter too."

"I never heard none," said Rick, "but I'll try."

They perched themselves on a rail fence, where the road made a bend in plain view of Harm Higgins' house. The hounds and Old Gum lay down quietly.

"What's that house all lit up for?" asked Billy.

"Golly!" said Glen. "I clear forgot. Higgins' wife died today, Mammy said. All the neighbors is there, settin' up all night."

"They say painters like to hang round where somebody's dead," said Rick, laughing. "A good chance to scare all them folks. I'll just see what I can do." He let out a high-pitched cry which shivered with a long-drawn-out tremolo.

"Golly, that was wonderful, Rick!" said Billy.

"Hit sounded just like a woman a-screamin'. That's the way a painter does hit, I heard Pap say," added Glen.

"Looky! Looky!" cried Jack, pointing to the house.

They saw the door open and a shaft of light shine out. They saw a number of people come out on the porch to listen.

"I'd better give 'em somethin' more to hear," said Rick. He gave his cry again, loud and long.

"Let's run," said Jack, "afore some o' them men come to shoot the painter."

So they all ran. "We'll make for Jeff Allison's farm now," said Rick, "where the pig was killed."

They cut across several cornfields and pastures, and came within sight of the Allison house. Rick wailed his panther cry again.

Allison's dog came running out, barking furiously. Glen held the dogs back and told them to keep quiet. Allison's dog sniffed around a bit, then ran back to the house.

"Hit's that painter again," they heard Allison say, as he stood on his front porch. "The dog's smelled hit, and hit's scared the gizzard outa him!" He took the dog indoors and soon the light in the window went out.

"Jeff ain't takin' no chances when there's a painter loose," laughed Rick. "He's goin' straight to bed, him and his dog."

"Let's give him somethin' to see when he gets up in the mornin'," said Jack. "Let's show him the painter's been here."

They took out their knives and made scratches on some fence

[ 164 ]

rails, throwing several down on the ground. They scratched the bark of a tree to imitate the work of a panther's claws.

"Why don't he come out and shoot it, when hit's scared his dog so bad?" asked Glen.

"Oh golly, we better go, afore he starts shootin'," said Billy.

"Likely he ain't got no gun or pistol," said Rick. "He'll come over tomorrow to try to borry some from Pappy. And Pappy'll lend him some, and he'll get all the men on the mountain out a-chasin' a booger painter!"

The boys roared with laughter. Then, to offset suspicion, in case Jeff might have heard them, Rick let out another wailing cry. After that, they ran.

They started off with the dogs down the slope of Ivy Mountain, and up through the woods to find the cave on Laurel. Halfway up, they stopped and greedily ate all the food they had brought with them. It was slow going. The night was dark, there was no moon, and the lantern made only a feeble light. They stumbled along through brush and thicket, trying to find a trail. Sometimes they nearly lost the old dog, Gum, who lumbered along slowly behind them, tired and sleepy.

"There's wild turkeys and wild hogs up here," said Rick. "Plenty chestnuts and beechnuts for 'em to eat."

"Let's shoot us a hog and take hit home and dress hit and have streaked middlin' for breakfast," said Jack.

"Shucks!" said Glen. "I'd druther ketch us a bear while we're at it."

"Ain't that the Drop-Off up there?" asked Billy, pointing to a vague form outlined against the sky.

"Hit shore looks like it," said Jack. "I'm a-gittin' tired. I'm 'bout ready to rest my bones a while."

"There's plenty bears in them thickets near the Drop-Off . . ." began Glen.

"Hush up!" whispered Rick, who was going ahead. "I heard voices. There's somebody around here somewheres. Put out the lantern. Get your guns ready."

"Golly, are we gonna shoot a bear?" asked Glen.

"Maybe hit's the painter," said Billy.

"Painters don't *talk!*" said Rick.

"Let out your yell," said Jack. "That'll scare 'em and they'll run."

"Golly, no!" whispered Billy. "I nigh forgot. Boys, there's a still round here somewheres. Granny Trivett told me. Said hit was a mighty good place to locate a still, close to the Tennessee line."

Billy's cousins crowded round him, to hear all he knew.

"If we could ketch some moonshiners," said Jack, "likely we'd get a big reward."

"How much do you reckon they'd pay?" asked Glen.

"Huh!" snorted Rick. "Got to ketch 'em first—if they don't shoot you. Maybe a dollar then."

"We got shootin'-irons, ain't we?" said Jack.

"Just two," said Rick.

"But we won't shoot 'em, will we?" asked Billy. "Then how could we get our reward?"

"Where is this still, Billy?" demanded Rick.

"Aw, I don't know," said Billy. "Like as not Granny Trivett was just makin' hit up to scare me. Said hit was in No Man's Cove."

"Over this way then," said Rick. "Let's head for Bearskin Creek. I hear water drippin' and runnin'. Come on."

But Billy did not move.

"Rick!" he called in a frantic whisper. "I see somebody up there on the Drop-Off!"

"Maybe hit's the painter," said Jack. "That's where the rock cave is. Git your guns ready."

"I shore would like to shoot a bear," said Glen.

"Hit ain't a painter nor a bear," whispered Billy. "Hit's a man. I seen his hat, and he's got a gun."

"We'll hide right here," whispered Rick. "Git down, all of you."

They lay down on the ground, and held the dogs to keep them from barking. Soon they heard men's voices, and footsteps close at hand in the brush, instead of up on the Drop-Off. The moon came up over the valley, and by its light they saw a group of three men pass. The boys raised themselves and stared.

"Hit looked like Walt Moseley," said Rick, after the men had disappeared.

"But he lives way over on Three Top," said Billy. "Who were the others?"

"Pappy Weaselface," said Jack, "shore as the hair on a hog's hide."

"And Joe Farley," said Glen. "Three of a kind—from Buckwheat Holler."

"Let's foller 'em to their still," said Rick.

It was a rough and almost impassable trail, crossing Bearskin Creek and going for nearly a mile to No Man's Cove. Hearing the men talking ahead, the boys stopped abruptly. They hid behind a rock to see what the men were doing. An ox-team was hitched to a wagon, and the wagon was loaded with tubs, copper boilers, copper tubing, kegs and buckets. Shadowy figures of men were loading more things on.

"Is it the Law—cuttin' up the still?" whispered Billy.

"No," answered Rick. "They'd be choppin' hit up with axes. Hit ain't the Law. Hit's the owners. They're movin' the still.

[ 168 ]

Maybe they been told on. They're gettin' away while gettin's good."

"Hush!" warned Glen. "They'll hear us."

The men climbed on the wagon and drove off.

"Let's foller 'em," said Jack, "and see where they're goin'."

The wagon made noise enough to cover the sound of their footsteps, so there was no longer need for caution. The valley road in No Man's Cove led in only one direction—over Stone Mountain to Tennessee. "They're goin' over the state line to be safe," said the boys. So they turned back.

"If only we'd come a mite sooner," said Jack, "we might could a got a reward."

"We'll go up on the Drop-Off and see if that painter's there," said Rick.

"I druther shoot me a bear," persisted Glen.

"Golly, let's sleep somewheres," said Jack. "I'm mighty doggone tired."

They lumbered back up to the ridge, climbing and scaling rocks, and pushing thick bushes aside. They entered the cave, but there was no panther waiting for them, and no bear either. They came out on the Drop-Off, a huge cliff which jutted out over steep rocks below. A cold wind blew up from the valley.

"Let's sleep out here," said Rick.

"Law, no," said Billy. "Hit's too cold. Hit might snow."

Just then he saw it. Beyond a clump of bushes at one side, Billy saw something moving. Was it the panther? He pointed, speechless.

"Golly! I seen something move!" gasped Rick. "The painter!"

The boys huddled together. It was darker now. The animal stayed motionless behind a big-leaved rhododendron bush. Then suddenly it moved and came toward them. They were too scared to run.

Then they saw that it had a hat on. It was a man. Old Gum growled.

"Howdy, boys!" the man said.

"Gosh Almighty!" gulped Billy. "Hit's Pap!"

CHAPTER XII

# Big Fat Possum

RUDOLPHUS HONEYCUTT stepped out in the moonlight which now flooded the Drop-Off.

"What you boys doin' out here in the middle of the night?" he demanded. "Up to some o' your gamesome tricks?"

Billy could not speak. He could not very well tell his father about the panther which did not exist, nor about camping out all night, because they hadn't camped at all. There was nothing left but the still, and maybe the still was Pappy's . . . his old fear returned.

"There's a still down in No Man's Cove," began Rick.

"The men are movin' hit over into Tennessee, Pap," Billy blurted out. "We seen 'em go in their wagon."

"Just what I wanted to know," said Pappy. "You needn't

tell me who they are—I know. I gave 'em their orders—to clear out afore the moon came out tonight, or else——"

"You told 'em to go, Pap? How'd you find out they had their still there?" asked Billy, his heart suddenly lightened.

"Why, young un, I knowed hit all along," said Pap. "I told 'em six months ago to get movin' and I been keepin' my eye on 'em ever since."

"But Granny Trivett 'lowed as you——"

"She told you I was a moonshiner?" asked Pap smiling.

"She didn't rightly know for sure," said Billy, "but I reckon she thought so."

"She knew too much about the whole thing," said Pappy. "I was afraid she'd make trouble for Walt and Pappy and Joe, and I wanted them to have the chance to move out before somebody told on 'em and brought the Law on 'em. That's why I tried to move her somewheres else, but your Mammy put a stop to that. I was afeared Granny would go blabbin'."

"Law, no, Pap, the best thing she does is keep her mouth shut tight," said Billy. "She learned Sarey Sue and me to do hit too."

"Can you boys all keep your mouths shut tight?" asked Pappy.

"Shore can," said the boys.

"The still's gone," said Pappy, "and I hope that's the last we'll see of Walt Moseley and his gang."

"What about Burl?" asked Billy.

"Gone too. Whole family's movin' to Tennessee," said

Pappy, "but don't say nothin' about hit."

"Shucks! No more fightin' for me to do!" laughed Billy.

Pappy turned to Rick, Glen and Jack. "Hit's a fur piece back to Last Hope Holler, boys," he said. "Hit's cloudin' and fixin' to snow before mornin'. Come down home with Billy and me and we'll find you some beds."

They were all dead tired and bed sounded good. Rick let out his shivering tremolo cry, for sheer delight.

Pappy said, "You sound just like a painter, Rick!" and wondered why the boys laughed so loud.

The next morning the ground was covered with snow, and Uncle Jamie's boys left for home right after a late breakfast. When they were gone, Mammy spoke up:

"The hens made a terrible squallin' last night. Sounded like hit might be a possum. What about that new pup—ain't he s'posed to keep possums away?"

"Come on, Banjo, let's go see," called Billy.

Billy understood many things about his father that had puzzled him before. Pappy had been trying to get rid of the still without doing harm to anybody. What a difference it made! Billy forgot how he had hated the hound pup.

It was easy to see tracks in the new-fallen snow. The dog sniffed and became excited. He followed the tracks which led from the chicken coop down to the branch, where a large dead chestnut log lay. The bole of the tree was rotten and had a hollow in it. Billy looked closely. Something had crawled up into it.

The dog sniffed, jumped up on the log and began to bark.

Billy patted him on the head. "Just wait, Banjo," he said. "Wait till I get me a stick. Down in that big wad o' leaves, there's the biggest ole possum you ever saw in the warmest ole bed. He's a mean fellow to bite and I don't want to get bit."

Billy stirred the leaves with his stick. Banjo kept on barking. Suddenly Billy pulled the possum out with a quick jerk of its hard, smooth tail, and dropped it. The small furry animal lay on the ground, perfectly still. Banjo stood by, waiting for it to show signs of life, so he could nab it.

"Good dog!" There was Pappy, come out to watch. "A born possum dog, I told you so."

Pappy held out a meal sack and Billy rolled the possum into it. "Take hit in the house and show hit to your Mammy."

Billy took the sack over his shoulder and went in. Red Top and Mazie were playing *William Tremble Toe* on the hearth. Letty Jo was hanging pumpkin rings and gourds on a long pole to dry.

"What you got, Billy?" asked Red Top.

"Live possum," said Billy.

"What you fixin' to do with hit?"

"Turn hit loose by the fire to get warm," laughed Billy. He opened the mouth of the sack and dumped the animal out. The possum rolled over on the hearth, close to the fire.

"Hit's dead, the possum's dead!" shouted Red Top, dancing about.

"Him dead! Him dead!" echoed Mazie.

"He's only pretending—just playin' possum," said Billy. "Mammy, come see how fat hit is—Banjo's first possum."

"Hit's a sight!" exclaimed Mammy. "Been feedin' off my fat hens, no wonder. Did you find hit asleep in my chicken nestes?"

Letty Jo reached up to hang her pole above the fireplace. "Shucks! Git out o' here." She gave the animal a playful kick. "Git outa here afore I step on you, you little ole varmint."

The smell of singed fur spread through the room.

"Tote that varmint right out o' this-here house!" ordered Mammy. "Hit's burnin' all hit's fur off."

"I'll kill it," said Pappy, "and we'll have roast possum for dinner."

"I ain't cookin' no possum," said Mammy firmly.

"Billy can skin the hide," added Pappy, "and make hisself a warm winter cap."

"Don't kill him," said Billy. "He's a real cute little feller."

"Tote that varmint out o' this-here house, I said," ordered Mammy.

Billy took the possum out in the yard and turned the heavy iron washpot over it. The next day, when he went out to look, it had dug out from under the pot and was gone.

The morning was cold and Mammy was cross. "Go git us in some wood, you young uns, afore we freeze to death," she

[ 175 ]

said. "There's nary a stick in the yard nor on the porch."

"Letty Jo," said Pappy, sitting down by the warm fire, "you and Billy take the gray mule and git up some wood. There's an old chestnut down up in the holler and there's a couple green hickories over in the pasture beyond them slick rocks you can chop."

The boy and girl started out with Old Bet, taking a logging chain with grappling hooks on it. Banjo went along. Billy chopped the trees and they fastened them together one after the other, behind Old Bet. It began to snow heavily. Billy had to keep whacking the mule to get the load down the mountain-side.

Banjo stopped and began to bark. Boney Old Bet stopped too, to rest. "Maybe hit's another possum," said Billy.

The dog jumped on top of an old stump, barking. The stump had a rotten hole in it.

"There's a possum down in them there leaves," said Billy, "as shore as a hound dog's got fleas."

"Who cares about possums, nohow?" said Letty Jo. She ran on to the house to warm her cold hands. It had stopped snowing, but the sky looked dark and heavy.

"You'd ought to be glad to have a sure-enough possum dog like Banjo," said Pappy, who just came up. "He don't need no trainin'. He's takened it up hisself. I knew he had it in him when I seen him first as a pup. You'd ought to be glad to have a good possum dog like that, son."

"Is he *my* dog?" asked Billy, in surprise. "Banjo?"

"Reckon so," said Pappy. "Hit was your money paid for him."

Billy had grown fond of the pup in spite of himself. He had liked having the pup around. He had even learned to call him by name, without feeling a sense of loss for the banjo he never got. He hadn't told any one, but Banjo had already formed a habit of sleeping on the foot of his bed at night. How could he go on hating a dog like that?

He understood now, too, why Pappy liked dogs so much— better than music, which he did not understand. Pappy was a real hunter, even though he had to work at farming and logging to support his family. And Billy was a hunter too. No mountain man or boy could be anything but a hunter at heart. And to a hunter, a dog was more to be desired than anything else in the world. Hunters just had to have dogs. They'd pay good money for dogs, even when they didn't have enough to eat.

Billy put his arms around Banjo and hugged him tight. The dog looked up expectantly, waiting for orders from the boy. He seemed to know he belonged to Billy.

The boy poked the possum out of his hole with a stick.

"Hit's playin' dead, Banjo. Don't touch."

Banjo sniffed and stood still, wagging his tail.

"Why, hit's the same possum we had in the house," said Billy. "Look, Pappy, hit's got the fur singed off on one side."

"Same identical varmint," said Pap. "Want me to kill hit?"

"Law, no," said Billy. "I got an i-dee. Me and Banjo'll go over and take hit to Uncle Pozy. He's the craziest man over possum in the whole county. We'll take hit to him."

"Good," said Pappy. "But not till we get this wood drug in and cut up. Your Mammy's fair freezin' to death."

"Reckon Banjo could *tree* a possum, Pappy?" asked Billy.

"Shore could," answered his father. "He could smell a possum a mile off."

Billy put the possum in a meal sack and kept it there while he helped saw up the trees. Letty Jo took one end of the cross-cut saw and Billy the other. As the short stove-length pieces fell, Mammy stood them on end and split them with the two-bitted axe. Mazie and Red Top carried the pieces and stacked them on the back porch outside the kitchen door. Now the

family could be warm again—until the wood was used up.

The next morning Billy threw the possum sack over Old Bet's back and set out for Honeysuckle Hollow. He kept whistling to Banjo, who followed along behind.

Uncle Pozy was standing just inside the door, working. With long white-oak splits, he was weaving back and forth, making a sturdy bottom for a handmade chair.

"Hello!" called Billy, running up on the porch.

Uncle Pozy dropped everything.

"Great groundhogs! If hit ain't Billy Honeycutt!" he cried, delighted. "Set down and rest yourself. Here—lemme find you a chair."

"See what I brung you, Uncle Pozy," said Billy. He opened the meal sack and dumped the possum out. "My dog ketched hit," he said proudly, "my dog, Banjo." He patted the dog beside him, on the head.

"You got a dog? And his name's Banjo? and that's *him*?" Uncle Pozy stared at the dog.

Billy had a lot of explaining to do.

"Jumpin' grasshoppers!" exclaimed Uncle Pozy. "If that ain't the beatin'est! You got a dog o' your very own, and you brung me the very first possum he ever ketched. Well now, if I ain't the tickledest man this side o' Tennessee!" He patted the dog on the head, then examined the possum. "Fattest ole possum in the county, ain't hit? Now, if there's anything I relish, hit's a bait o' possum meat."

"Mammy won't never cook hit at our house," said Billy.

"Women-folks has funny notions, sometimes," said Uncle

[ 180 ]

Pozy. "I'll tell you what I always do first, son. I put the possum up in a good strong pen, where it can't get out or burrow out, and I fatten hit up on good, clean feed for about ten days . . . and then I cook hit just right to make hit tasty. Looky here, son, all the fur's gone off one side."

Billy explained what had happened. Then he added: "You're gonna mess around with hit till hit bites you, Uncle Pozy."

The ole man kept on feeling round the possum's neck and back of its head. Then suddenly, "Ouch!" he screamed. "Wicked little varmint, you! Out in your pen you go!"

It was a long time since Billy had been to Uncle Pozy's. It seemed good to be there again and talk with the old man. The

boy took up a long split of white oak and began to weave it in and out through the chair bottom.

"You come too late for dinner, son," said Uncle Pozy, "but I got somethin' for you to eat all the same." He put beans and stewed apples and corn-bread on the table and pressed the boy to eat. He found some bones for Banjo. He was bubbling with happiness over Billy's return.

"How come you're not makin' baskets, Uncle Pozy?" asked Billy with his mouth full.

"That Miz Sutherland's takened it into her head to buy some handmade chairs," explained Uncle Pozy. "So I started makin' 'em again. Whenever I get tired makin' baskets, I make chairs for a change."

"You got plenty work to do to make a good livin', ain't you, Uncle Pozy?" said Billy. He remembered how Jeb Dotson had accused him of running Uncle Pozy out of business, and he wanted to be reassured.

"More'n I can do," said the old man, "and all off my own place. Did you ever think when you was walkin' through the woods that there was baskets and chairs a-growin' right there afore your eyes?"

Billy nodded, his mouth full of corn-bread. "And calico dresses and banjos, too," he mumbled softly, but the old man did not hear.

"Shall we have us a little music?" asked Uncle Pozy, when Billy had finished eating He looked toward his dulcimer, but hesitated to take it down.

"Oh Uncle Pozy, I ain't told you," cried Billy, jumping up. "Uncle Jamie's learnin' me to play the fiddle! I'm goin' over two-three times a week to take lessons. Mammy said I might could, now there ain't so much work to do come winter."

"Lordy mercy!" cried Uncle Pozy. "Think o' that now!"

"None of Uncle Jamie's boys take to hit like I do, he says," Billy went on. "He wants me to come as often as I can." The boy paused. "But I don't know what Pap'll say when he finds out—he 'lows as music don't grow corn and beans."

"Likely your Pap'll change his mind," said the old man.

"And say, Uncle Pozy," cried Billy again, "Pap didn't have nothin' to do with that still in No Man's Cove, after all."

"Shoo, now," said Uncle Pozy, "of course not. Your Pappy's a good man and a law-abiding citizen. I knowed that all along."

"The still's gone now," said Billy, "and I'm powerful glad. The folkses that owned it—Pappy said I'd better not tell their names. . . ."

"Law no, I don't want to know who they were," said Uncle Pozy.

"They come and drug hit over the hills into Tennessee," said Billy. "Pap and I seen 'em go, in the middle of the night."

"You was with your Pap? He takened you? And you talked this all over with him?"

Billy nodded. "Law, yes."

"That's good. Now you can trust your Pap again," said Uncle Pozy.

"And Granny Trivett and Sarey Sue can roam all over the mountain in peace," said Billy.

"They didn't bother her none, I hope," said Uncle Pozy.

"Law, no," said Billy. "Gran was too smart for 'em. She knew all about hit, but wouldn't say a word."

"I hear she owns the whole mountain," laughed Uncle Pozy.

"I reckon she does," said Billy.

Uncle Pozy took down his dulcimer.

"First, let me put Banjo out the door," laughed Billy. "He don't like music as much I do. He'll howl!"

The old man touched the strings and sang softly:

"Down in the valley, the valley so low,
Hang your head over, hear the winds blow;
Hear the winds blow, dear, hear the winds blow,
Hang your head over, hear the winds blow.

If you don't love me none else will do,
My heart is breaking, dear, just for you,
Breaking for you, dear, breaking for you,
My heart is breaking, dear, just for you.

Roses love sunshine, violets love dew,
Angels in heaven knows I love you,
Knows I love you dear, knows I love you,
Angels in heaven knows I love you . . ."

CHAPTER XIII

## *A Letter for Billy*

M EAL'S a gettin' low," said Mammy, after breakfast. It
was six o'clock and the morning was cold. Winter
had come to Hoot Owl Hollow.

"Go get that drag and bring in a load o' corn, son," said
Pappy.

Billy dumped the corn on the hearth in the front room.
Everybody sat down by the firelight and began to shuck and
shell the corn. Even Mazie and Red Top helped.

Soon Billy started, his sacks of corn lying over the gray
mule's back, riding off to mill. He buttoned his coat tightly
across his chest, and rubbed his hands together to warm them.

The rutty road that followed Roundabout Creek was rough
and frozen now. In shallow places in the creek, ice could be

seen. The mail-wagon had just arrived from Cranberry, so Billy decided not to stop at the post office until he returned.

"Had any fights lately?" chuckled Old Hamby at the mill.

"Not since the Moseleys left," answered Billy. He waited leisurely while the old wheel creaked and churned, grinding the corn.

"Whoa, mule! Whoa, I say!" Billy jumped down and went into the post office to warm himself. The tiny stove was red hot.

"Ary letter for me, Miss Viney?"

Miss Viney held a letter in her hand. "Now who," she asked in a teasing voice, "could be writing to Bill Honeycutt, I wonder?" She gazed at the letter through her spectacles.

"Hit can't be for *me*," said Billy. "You're foolin', Miss Viney. I don't know ary soul in all the world who'd write me a letter."

"You don't?" Miss Viney's long thin arm came slowly out the little window. She smiled happily, as Billy took the letter.

Billy stared at it. He had never had a letter before in his life. But there was his name, printed on the front in big letters: Billy Honeycutt, Solitude, N. C. He was the only Billy Honeycutt in Solitude.

"Who's it from, Billy?" asked Miss Viney.

"Danged if I know!" he answered.

Then before the postmistress could ask any more questions, he flung himself on Old Bet's back and went flying up the creek.

"Mammy! Pappy! Letty Jo!" he called. "I got me a letter!"

"Whoever from?" asked Letty Jo.

"I had a cousin livin' in Georgia once . . ." began Mammy.

"And what was the name of that Uncle o' mine up in Virginy?" asked Pappy.

Mammy and Pappy looked at each other and smiled.

"Open hit!" demanded Red Top, standing on a chair.

"Let's hear what hit says," added Letty Jo. "Then we'll know who writ it."

With shaky fingers, Billy tore the envelope open. He read the letter through, then he looked up, with disappointment on his face.

"Hit's a mistake," he said. "Hit ain't for me, after all. Hit's from a mail-order house in Chicago. Hit's about an 'order for goods' that somebody sent 'em. Hit says they'll send hit soon, by express, to the depot at Cranberry. Hit ain't for me. I ain't ordered nothin'."

Pappy looked at Mammy. "Never heard o' no other Billy Honeycutt in Solitude, did you?"

"Never did." Mammy covered her mouth with her apron quickly. Was she laughing or crying?

The mysterious letter lay on the table. Three days later, Pappy returned from Cranberry and lifted a large box out of the jolt-wagon.

"Why, hit's from Chicago, and here's my name on hit!" exclaimed Billy.

"Open hit! Open hit!" demanded Red Top.

They all crowded round while Pappy opened the box on Christmas day, and Mammy took the things out one by one. There was a doll with golden hair for Mazie, a little red wagon for Red Top, a new shirt for Pappy, gay red suspenders for Pappy and Billy, and several lengths of pretty dress-goods for new dresses for Mammy and Letty Jo. Then, down at the bottom, lay a mysterious object, well-packed and padded. Pappy took it out and laid it carefully on the table.

"Open hit, son," he said. Billy opened the wrappings.

There lay a beautiful, shiny violin.

It was too beautiful to touch or talk about. Even Red Top and Mazie said not a word.

"There must be some other Billy Honeycutt somewheres . . ." said the boy when he could find words. "This ain't for me——"

"Yes, son, hit's your'n," said Pappy.

"For me to play on?"

"Better to take lessons on your *own* fiddle instead o' your

Uncle Jamie's," said Pappy. "I hear these fiddlers are partial to an instru-ment o' their very own."

Still Billy did not understand. What had made Pap change his mind like this?

"Music don't grow corn and beans," said the boy in a low voice.

"Tell him, Rudy," said Mammy.

"Hit's all on account o' that hound pup you got this fiddle," said Pappy.

"Don't pester him, Rudy," said Mammy. "He's waited so long. Tell him."

"What's Banjo got to do with it?" asked Billy.

"Hit was this way," said Pappy. "I met Uncle Pozy down

to the store one day and we got to talkin' about that hound pup o' your'n. I says what a good possum dog he is, and Uncle Pozy says how good that big fat possum tasted. I says: 'The pup's just got it *in* him—he's a born possum dog, can't help hisself.' Then Uncle Pozy says: 'Just like that boy o' your'n. He's got music in his blood. You can't stamp hit out. He's a born musician if ever I see one.' "

"Uncle Pozy said that?" asked Billy.

"Yes, son," said Pappy. "I hadn't never thought about hit that way before, but that blamed possum dog made me see it."

Billy bent over and patted Banjo on the head.

"So when I sold that last load o' logs," Pappy went on, "I made up my mind my boy should have instru-ment of his own. And your Mammy was needin' right smart other things and Christmas was a-comin' . . . ."

"So we sent to the mail-order house to get 'em," added Mammy.

Billy took his eyes off the new fiddle and looked at the pretty lengths of dress-goods. "How many new dresses you gonna have, Letty Jo?"

His sister tossed her head. "Two-three, I reckon."

Billy touched a piece with a flowered pattern. "I wisht . . . ."

"What is it, son?" asked Mammy.

"Sarey Sue ain't never had no new dress with purties on hit. Granny makes her wear old brown linsey all the time . . . ."

Mammy folded up the piece Billy had chosen. "We got more'n we need. You take this un to Sarey Sue."

Billy hesitated. "Is hit calico? Are you shore hit's calico?"

Mammy fingered the piece. "Hit's better'n calico. Hit's *lawn,* that piece, flowered lawn."

"I'll take hit to her," said Billy. He started out the door.

When he reached the Half-Way-Up House, Sarey Sue and Granny were sitting beside the fire and Sarey Sue was playing her accordion. There was music and cheer, without loneliness, on Christmas day, in the little cabin on the side of the mountain.

Sarey Sue came running out when she heard Billy calling. "We got us a new cow-brute!" she shouted, pointing to the shed.

"Who cares about a new cow-brute?" answered Billy. "Here's a new dress—get busy with your finger-sewin', gal. Get ready to make all them teeny-tiny stitches. I hear they had a square dance down at Jasper Jackson's house last Saturday night and had 'em a big time. Fix up your new dress and you can go to the next one."

Sarey Sue opened her mouth to speak, but no words came.

"Where'd you get hit?" demanded Granny. "You ain't stole hit from Jeb Dotson's store?"

"Jeb ain't got no purties like this, Gran," said Sarey Sue.

"Pap sent a big order to the mail-order house in Chicago," said Billy, "and got something nice for all of us for Christmas —and this purty dress for Sarey Sue. Guess what he got for me?"

The two stared at the boy.

"A fiddle!" he cried. His face shone with happiness.

"From Chicago?" gasped Granny. "A fotched-on fiddle?"

"Law, yes," said Billy. "Hit's so purty, I'm skeered to touch it."

"Lordy mercy, what's the world a-comin' to!" said Granny. "A fotched-on fiddle for Billy and a store-bought calicker dress for Sarey Sue. Glory be!"

"'Taint calicker, Gran," said the girl, her voice full of awe.

"Hit's *lawn,* Mammy said," explained Billy. "Lawn's bet-ter'n calico."

*"Lawn!"* echoed Sarey Sue. "Blamed stuff's so thin you can see smack dab through it." She looked at Billy and added: "Guess your Pappy's not mean after all."

It was a month later when word came of Uncle Jamie's acci-dent. Cousin Rick rode over to Hoot Owl Hollow one Sunday to bring the news.

"Hit was that new colt he was tryin' to break," explained Rick. "She was plenty wild and she throwed him. His right arm's broke in two places and he can't play the fiddle with his arm in a sling."

"Shore is too bad," said Mammy.

"What can we do to help?" asked Pappy.

"Us boys can carry on the farm work," said Rick, "but there's that square dance comin' off in Jasper Jackson's house on Saturday night next week. Pappy 'lowed as Billy might could play some o' them fiddle tunes he's been a-learnin' him."

[ 193 ]

"Me?" asked Billy. "Me play for the square dance?"

"Law yes, you, son," said Mammy, putting her arm around the boy's shoulder. "You're never too young to begin. If Uncle Jamie says you can, then you can."

"There ain't nobody else in these parts, Pappy said," added Rick.

Billy turned to Pappy. "Can I do hit, Pap?" he asked.

"Reckon so," said Pappy, smiling. "They can't have a square dance without a fiddler. What's that new fiddle for, nohow?"

Billy breathed deeply. He could hardly believe it was Pappy talking.

"Pap says you're to come over every day to practice on his fiddle," said Rick. "He'll lend it to you for the dance. He'll do the callin', even if his arm is in a sling."

"Ain't you heard? I got my *own* fiddle, Rick!" said Billy proudly.

When Rick saw the beautiful violin lying in its case, his eyes nearly popped out of his head. So Billy explained.

"Don't you-uns dare touch hit!" warned Red Top.

"Gosh almighty, you ain't even touched hit yet?" gasped Rick.

"I couldn't touch hit the first day," admitted Billy. "After that I just had to hear it singin' . . ."

He picked up the fiddle and played *Sourwood Mountain* right through.

"Golly!" said Rick. "Sounds just like Pappy."

"The hounds don't like hit," said Letty Jo. "They howl their heads off when Billy gets to practisin' his lively tunes."

"But *we* like hit!" cried Mazie and Red Top, holding hands and dancing around the room.

The night of the square dance, everybody came to Jasper Jackson's house. The beds had been taken down and the furniture moved out of the big front room. All the neighbors were there—the Holbrooks, the Wilcoxes, Old Hamby and his niece's family, Jeb Dotson, the Wileys, the Allisons and many others. When the Trivetts came in, Sarey Sue became the center of interest, she looked so pretty in her new flowered lawn dress.

"Lordy mercy!" cackled Granny Trivett, "what a crowd! I ain't seen the like since I was a gal young un myself, the age of Sarey Sue." Granny's eyes moved slowly round the room. "I see everybody here but the Moseleys. Lizy ain't worse off, be she? They ain't sent for me lately. . . ."

Nobody answered. Some of the women began whispering to each other.

"Anything happened to the Moseleys?" asked Granny in a loud voice. "Lizy ain't dead, and nobody told me?"

No one replied.

Granny's eye fell on Billy Honeycutt. He was dressed in a new suit, and wore brand-new bright red suspenders. "You ain't fit Burl Moseley lately, have you, Billy?"

"Law, no," answered the boy. He edged up close and said in a whisper: "Ain't you heard, Granny?"

"No, heard what? Nobody ain't told me nothin'."

Billy turned to his mother. "Gran ain't heard about the Moseleys, Mammy."

"Come over here and set down, Granny," said Billy's mother.

They crowded close on the bench, Billy between them.

"There ain't no still in No Man's Cove no more," explained Billy in a whisper. "Pappy and I seen the men drag hit up over Stone Mountain one moonlight night—into Tennessee."

"Good riddance!" snorted Granny.

"Pap never run that still," said Billy.

"Why, I knowed that all along, son," said Granny.

"Hit was Walt Moseley and his gang," said Billy.

"I suspicioned as much," snorted Granny again. "I seen him a good many times too often on yon side o' Laurel Mountain."

"Poor Lizy," said Billy's mother. "I feel for her, followin' a man like Walt hither and yon, for better and for worse, till he gets caught."

"Wonder who'll take care of her over in Tennessee," said Granny.

"You done a plenty to keep her well," said Mammy, "always a-runnin' to her whenever she felt an ache or a pain."

Granny threw up her hands. "What else could a body do?"

"Time for the dancin' to begin!" called Uncle Jamie. "Come on, boys, do that hoe-down!"

He took Billy by the arm and stepped up to one end of the room. He explained to the crowd about his broken arm, and then went on: "Say, folks, let me introduce to you the fiddler of the evenin', whose name is . . . whose name is . . . well, we like to give fiddlers fancy names, so let's call him *Blue Ridge Billy!*"

Everybody laughed and clapped and stamped their feet. Billy blushed and hung his head.

"You have the chance, folks, to listen to Blue Ridge Billy's first public performance," Fiddlin' Jamie went on. "A few years from now, this young feller may surprise you by becom-

[ 197 ]

ing the Champion Fiddler o' the County . . . and after that, Champion o' North Caroliny, and after that, of the U. S. Nation!"

They all clapped and stamped again.

"But meanwhiles," added Fiddlin' Jamie, "if he makes a few mistakes, just don't pay 'em no mind. He ain't had too much time to practice up. All right, let's go. I'll do the callin', while Billy does the fiddlin'—a good ole mountain tune, *Soldier's Joy!* Get your partners. Form a ring! Count off! Start the music! All go left!"

Billy lifted his beautiful new fiddle to its place under his chin. It felt comfortable and so did the bow in his hand. As the fiddle began to sing, a great joy filled his heart. He forgot the frolicking people in front of him. His dream had come true at last.

"Promenade All!" Fiddlin' Jamie's calls rang out high over the music: "Right hands over, left hands back . . ." "Bird hop out and crow hop in . . ." "Ladies bow, gents know how . . ."

The dancing figures moved to the rhythm of Billy's music. The floor shook and the windows rattled, as the calls rang out and gay feet moved lightly over the rough pine floor.

The evening passed quickly for Billy.

He was conscious of other things besides the fiddle tunes which seemed to come out of their own accord. He could see his mother, sitting against the wall in the corner, smiling happily, with Mazie and Red Top asleep in her lap. Now and then he had a glimpse of Sarey Sue Trivett, dancing as she had never danced before, wearing a new dress all covered with "purties."

Then he saw that Granny Trivett had become the center of attention. She might be a hundred—nobody knew how old— but there she was, dancing and bowing and joining hands with Uncle Pozy, and hopping and tripping about as lively as young Sarey Sue. Everybody on the floor, even the dancers, watched her. When she sat down, breathless at last, they clapped and stamped until the walls of the building shook.

When the dancing was over, all the people, young and old, crowded round to praise Billy for his fiddling, and to tease Fiddlin' Jamie. "We don't need you no more, Jamie," they said. "We got us a better fiddler than you."

"Oh ho! When I learn this young ground hog all I know," retorted Fiddlin' Jamie, "maybe he'll be worth a dab o' grease."

Even Jeb Dotson came up to shake Billy's hand.

"Young feller," he said, "if I'd a knowed how bad you wanted that ere banjo, I'd a *give* hit to you. If I'd a knowed what a good player you'd be, I wouldn't a sold hit. . . ."

"Who did you sell it to?" asked Billy.

"That sorry little ole Burl Moseley," said Jeb. "Course I knowed he had his Pappy's git'-tar.... His fingers was good at pickin', but he never had wits enough to make a tune. He just ding-donged his Pappy till he got whatever he wanted outa him, and he wanted that ere banjo just to keep you from gettin' hit, and so his Pappy give me money——"

Billy turned away from him. He had heard enough.

Then Uncle Pozy came up, his round face wreathed in smiles.

"You've got music in your blood, son," he said gently, "like I been sayin' all along. You'll be a fiddler shore as water runs downhill. Your Pap believes hit now, don't he?"

Pappy stepped up. He had heard what Uncle Pozy said.

" 'Twas you set me right, Uncle Pozy," he replied, "just by talkin' about Billy's little ole possum dog. That was a new i-dee to me, but now I can see hit plain as the graveyard. This here boy can't keep from makin' music no more than that hound pup can stop ketchin' possums! Haw, haw!"

"Haw, haw, haw!" Uncle Pozy laughed too, and slapped Pappy on the back.

"That boy o' mine's the workin'est boy in the holler," Pappy went on. "He'll make a better farmer than his Pap, if he does some fiddlin' now and then."

"Wait till all them city folks come a-runnin' to hear this boy fiddle," said Uncle Jamie. "He'll make *Blue Ridge Billy* a name to be proud of."

Billy hung his head. He was not used to praise.

Then suddenly, Sarey Sue was there beside him.

"Remember my quilt-top, Billy? Remember what I said to you that day?"

Billy nodded. He could not trust himself to speak.

Then Sarey Sue added softly, "A dream's just *obliged* to come true, ain't hit?"

## The End

# MOUNTAIN WORDS AND PHRASES

Many words used in the Southern Highlands are pure "Old English" forms, called Anglo-Saxon—words used by Chaucer and Shakespeare. They have been handed down by word of mouth from Elizabethan days and earlier. The speech of the mountain people is not "poor English," but good *Old* English. It has been preserved in the mountains, but has been allowed to die out in other parts of our country.

*air*—are or is
*argify*—argue
*ary* (pronounced "air-y")—any

*a bait of meat*—a taste of
*baitin' trouble*—making trouble
*banjer*—banjo
*bestir*—stir up, rouse
*bide*—to stay
*biggety*—over-proud
*biscuit-bread*—soda biscuits
*bitty, little*—little bit of
*booger man*—a haunt or ghost
*bull nettle*—plant with prickly thorns
*burl, laurel*—the knotty root of a wild rhododendron bush

*case-knife*—table knife
*clift*—cliff
*corn-shucks*—husks of corn
*cow-brute*—cow
*cow-chop*—cow feed
*a-cravin*—wanting badly
*critter*—animal

*darst*—dare
*ding-donged*—annoyed
*down the country*—the level land below the mountains

*I druther*—I'd rather

*evenin'*—afternoon or evening

*fetch*—to go and bring something back
*fit*—fought, had a fight
*fore day*—morning
*fotched-on*—brought on from somewhere else
*nigh in a franzy*—worried
*a fur piece*—a long way
*furrin'*—foreign

*gall*—impudence, nerve
*gallivantin'*—roaming for pleasure
*gamesome*—mischievous, out for a good time
*git-tar*—guitar
*grub with a maddick*—to dig with a mattock or a digging tool
*grubbin'*—digging

*hankerin'*—wanting badly
*ha'nt*—ghost
*histed*—hoisted, lifted
*hit*—it
*holler, hollow*—valley between mountains
*holler*—to call out

*jolt-wagon*—farm wagon that jolts on rough country roads

*kin, kinfolks*—relatives
*knee-baby*—a walking baby

*law 'em*—bring a law-suit against
*leather-britches*—dried string beans
*light down*—to dismount from a horse
*light out*—to start out

*make a crop*—grow a crop
*make a stab*—try
*mammy* (pronounced "mom-my")—mother
*master hand for notions*—having fanciful ideas
*mosey*—to stroll or walk slowly
*muley cow*—a cow that never had any horns

*nag*—horse
*nigh*—near
*nigh in a franzy*—worried

*pappy* (pronounced "pop-py")—father·
*passel*—parcel, piece
*pizen*—poison
*to pleasure*—to please
*plumb purty*—very pretty
*plumb welcome*—very welcome
*plunder*—possessions
*poke*—sack or bag
*prankin'*—having fun
*purties*—flowers

*rabbity*—timid
*raggedy-drag*—ragged, unkempt

*relish*—like the taste of
*right smart*—a great deal
*rive shingles*—split shingles from a chunk of wood
*rock-house*—cave

*sassyfrack*—sassafras
*set a spell on*—to bewitch
*get shet of*—get rid of
*shootin' irons*—guns
*shore*—sure
*shucks*—husks of corn
*sight of money*—a great deal
*skedaddle*—run away quickly
*sleep in feathers*—sleep on a feather bed
*smack-dab*—exactly
*sorry*—of no account, not worth anything
*spindling*—thin and slender
*stay sot*—seated
*streaked middlin'*—lean bacon

*takened*—took
*tarry*—to stay at a place
*thickety*—thick and bushy
*this un*—this one
*tike*—mischievous, annoying child
*tote*—to carry
*traipsin'*—walking

*whole endurin' day*—all day long
*wildy*—grown wild
*'witchin'*—bewitching
*workin'est*—most industrious

*yarbin'*—digging roots and gathering herbs
*yarbs*—herbs
*you-uns*—you ones